*To Donna
It was [?]
to meet you.
Parker Kincade*

Spring Training
A GAME ON NOVEL

PARKER KINCADE

All rights reserved. No part of this publication may be reproduced, stored in a retrieval system, or transmitted in any form or by any means, electronic, mechanical, photocopying, recording or otherwise, without the prior written permission of the author.

Editor
Lacey Thacker

Cover Artist
Aimee Benson

Formatted by
JTLW Design

This is a work of fiction. The characters, incidents, places, brands and dialogues in this book are a product of the author's imagination and are used fictitiously. Any resemblance to actual events, or persons, living or dead, is completely coincidental.

This book contains content that is not suitable for readers who are 17 and under.

ISBN: 978-1489553805

Copyright © 2013 by Parker Kincade

DEDICATION

To Peg, for raising me, for always believing in me, and for being my biggest fan. I'm the person I am today because of you. I love you.

To Deni Golden, for your friendship and unwavering support. And for loving Garrett as much as I do!

And, of course, to Garrett. Your wicked smile and smooth southern charm get me every time.

ACKNOWLEDGEMENTS

There are so many people that helped put this book together and deserve recognition for their mad skills:

Lacey Thacker, thank you for all the writing dates, the reads and re-reads, and for doing the final editing. You're my peanut butter! JT Lacy, for being my technology guru, book formatter, all around go-to guy, and, most of all, for all the years of friendship you've blessed me with. Vanessa North, for the awesome cover. Monette Michaels, for being a great critique partner and not kicking my ass the first go-round. To all the ladies of the Diamond State Romance Authors for their support and counsel.

Mandy Harbin, thank you for your guidance, support and friendship. I don't know how I did all this before I met you.

Rome, my kids, Ty, and my entire family. You guys rock!

And finally, a special thanks to Brian Bednarz for naming my beloved New York Empire baseball team. Next beer is on me, brother!

CHAPTER ONE

Dread coursed through Jessa Montgomery's body. She rubbed her forehead, hoping like hell she wouldn't get a headache. She pressed her back against the cool concrete, its chill strangely soothing through her thin blouse.

She had no idea what she was doing here. Standing outside the locker room like a damn groupie. This wasn't her job. Her father, TJ Montgomery, owned the New York Empire major league baseball team. He had people to do this kind of thing. People that weren't her.

TJ was known for his unorthodox methods when it came to his players, treating them all like the favored sons he'd never had. He'd only had her. And even though he'd raised her in ballparks around the country, instilling his love for the game deep in her heart, she'd never quite felt as if she were enough.

And it still didn't explain why he'd sent her here. He'd been adamant that she not be directly involved with the players, and that suited her just fine. She knew the games men played. Especially those who were young, talented, and had their pick of women. Setting aside the fact that she had an uncanny ability to track talent and spot weaknesses in a player's game, Jessa preferred to be a behind-the-scenes kind of girl. Give her a game tape and a quiet office any day. She handled the administrative side of her father's life. She managed finances and paperwork from behind a desk. In New York.

She didn't attend spring training to babysit. Ever.

So, why this player? Why now?

One thing was for certain, TJ had never gotten as excited about anything Jessa had done as he was about the man she was here to meet. Her dad's new star player.

Jealousy left a bitter taste in her mouth as she glanced at her watch. A star player with a shitty sense of time.

Jessa inhaled deeply and rolled her eyes to the ceiling. God save her from spoiled athletes with more talent than sense. And damn her dad for putting her in the position to deal with a guy who probably thought the world revolved around him. They'd shelled out enough cash to fund a small country to make sure Garrett Donovan played for New York; the least he could do was show up on time.

Unable to stand still any longer, Jessa strolled up the tunnel, dragging her fingertips along the painted cinder blocks as she went. What the hell was she going to do? Keeping track of Garrett on the field was one thing, but off the field ... why the hell would her dad want her to keep an eye on his extracurricular activities? There were few who could match her knowledge of the game, but there had to be someone more qualified to deal with this man after-hours.

Jessa wasn't socially inept, but she chose to keep to herself. Her experience with men was limited, primarily because she hated being treated like a piece of meat. Female friendships were even harder to form. It seemed as if no one could look past her name or her dad's money to see who Jessa really was. Everyone wanted something from her. Call her cynical, but been there, done that.

Just once, she'd like to meet someone who would look past all that and realize there was so much more to her. But that wasn't going to happen this week. Not here and not in this place. Maybe not ever.

Which was why she'd prefer to spend every night in her hotel room, going over stats, preparing reports, hell, even watching a movie. Not keeping her dad's new best friend out of trouble. The last thing she wanted to do was subject herself to the wild Tampa nightlife. Whatever Garrett did in his spare time was his own business. She didn't want any part of it.

As much as she'd like to go with that, she knew it would never happen. What was it her dad had said?

"You're too much like me, baby girl. Focused. Driven. Responsible."

2

Translation? Boring. He'd made her sound like a damn car.

Yeah, she'd do her job. But if Garrett thought to drag her all over town while he played the night away, he had another thing coming.

As if she'd conjured him, the man in question rounded the corner, hesitating for a second when their eyes met. Tall and lean, with muscles that strained his practice uniform, Garrett Donovan was gorgeous. Sandy blond curls met the back of his collar, the mass of hair she'd seen in photos contained by the cap on his head. Crystal blue eyes gleamed against tanned skin as his lips turned up into the sexiest grin Jessa had never witnessed.

Holy shit.

His gaze burned a trail across her face, drinking her in before moving over the rest of her body. Her skin warmed under his perusal and she lifted her chin as he looked his fill. It wasn't something she'd normally tolerate, but the warmth in his eyes, the appreciation in his smile, didn't make her feel cheap. He'd made her feel beautiful.

What the heck was wrong with her?

She'd watched hours of footage of this man. Had watched the hard lines of his body as he swung a bat or fielded a ball. That man was nothing compared to the live and in person version walking toward her. She'd have to be dead not to notice his sensual energy, and her heart was beating just fine, thank you very much.

She needed to get a grip.

"Ms. Montgomery?" His smile filled with amusement as he extended his hand.

He knew his effect on her. The jackass was already trying to play her with his bedroom eyes and sultry smile. Like an idiot, she'd almost bought into it.

Jessa placed her hand in his and shook firmly, ignoring the jolt of awareness that sizzled up her arm, into her chest and straight to her nipples. "Mr. Donovan, you're late."

He nodded once, his hand lingering in hers. A hand that was large, warm, and tanned from long hours in the sun. He caressed her inner wrist and palm as he released her. "My apologies, Ms. Montgomery. I didn't realize you'd be waiting down here for me. Your father said —"

The mention of her dad ramped up her anger. "What's that supposed to mean? You think I've never been to a locker room before?"

He held his hands up, as if to defend himself. "Easy, princess. That's not what I meant at all."

Jessa squared her shoulders. "I'll have you know, I've spent more time on the dirt than you, so let's get one thing straight. I'm not your *princess*. My name is Jessa. And you owe me an apology. I've been waiting here for over an hour."

His lips thinned as he leaned against the wall. He crossed his arms over his chest, the muscled lines of his biceps straining his sleeves.

"All right, *Jessa*." His deep Southern drawl rolled over her. "How about we try this again. I'm Garrett. Sorry I'm late, but I have a good reason. If you're willing to hear it, that is."

Jessa was going to scream if he didn't stop staring at her as if he knew what she looked like naked. It made her want to show him, which wouldn't be good for either of them. She fisted her hands on her hips. "I'm sure I'll hear all about it on the six o'clock news. I hope you wore protection."

Jesus, what was wrong with her? She didn't give a shit who he got busy with. And she wasn't the kind of person to be rude to others. And yet ... "You should feel lucky I'm not going to fine you."

He shook his head, lazy smile back in place. "I never fuck without a glove, darlin', but thanks for the concern."

"Oh, my God, you did not just say that." She covered her face with her hands to hide her mortification. She'd never had a guy — a virtual stranger — talk to her that way before. Even if she had deserved it. If he'd meant to embarrass her, he'd succeeded.

"You're the one that brought it up. I was just trying to reassure you."

Her fingers itched to wipe that stupid grin off his face. Arrogant son of a bitch. "Just keep it off the news." She snapped.

"You think you've got me all figured out, don't you?"

She gave him a smile of her own, inwardly pleased when his eyes flared in response. "Let's see if I can get this right. Garrett Donovan, golden boy from Mississippi, played college ball for four years, forgoing early draft in lieu of receiving a degree in agriculture." She considered him. "Although I'm not sure why you would do that. Anyway, batting average four-hundred-and-three. You run the sixty in under six-point-three. You had twenty-three home runs, fifty-six RBI's and twenty-nine stolen bases your senior year alone. How am I doing so far?"

"Golden boy, huh?" His lips curled into a wicked grin. "You sure have a mess of stats in that pretty head of yours. What else ya got?"

Jessa bit back a smile. Oh, he was charming. Dangerous. The kind of man she should avoid. "You never used the standard aluminum bat, preferring the wooden bats you knew you'd be using if you got to the big club." Which, okay, impressed her a little. Not that she'd tell *him* that.

Before she could continue, Jim Freeman, longtime pitcher for the Empire, entered the tunnel. Jessa's tension eased somewhat as Jim strolled over, his gaze friendly and warm.

"Hi, Jessa." Jim held out his fist to Garrett. "What's up, G?"

Garrett fist bumped the guy. "Hey, Jim. How was the workout?"

"Brutal." Jim laughed. "I hear congratulations are in order."

Garrett actually beamed. "You got that right. Seven pounds, six ounces of beautiful baby girl." Their high-five resonated through the walkway.

Jessa stared in shock. Baby? What baby? Her brain rifled through all the information she had on Garrett and came up blank. No girlfriend that she'd heard about, and certainly no wife.

"Jessa?" Garrett was calling her name, waving his hand in front of her face.

"What? Sorry."

"Where'd you go?"

Her face heated again. She'd never blushed so much as in the last few minutes with this man. "Never mind. What were we talking about?" She ran her sweaty palms down the front of her shorts.

"You were thinkin' you had me all figured out." He was dangerously close to her now, one arm propped on the wall above her head.

When had he moved so close?

"I know what I need to know." She looked around for Jim, only to discover they were once again alone.

His laugh was deep, husky. "I guess we'll see about that." He leaned in, the rim of his cap teasing her hair. "You smell good. Like strawberries." His breath was warm against her face. "Makes me hungry."

Jessa couldn't control the shudder that traveled down her spine. Moisture pooled between her legs, her body practically begging to feed him.

Jessa was horrified by her response. He was just like all the rest. Flirting with her while his baby-mama was off taking care of their child.

She'd be damned if she'd become another of his conquests.

She offered him her sweetest smile, batting her eyelashes a few times for good measure. "Congratulations on your new baby, Garrett. When was she born?"

Garrett pushed away from her. That damned grin took her breath away.

"About ten hours ago. And she's my niece." His smile vanished. "My brother-in-law was killed in combat six months ago, so I had to be there to stand in with my sister. That's why I was late." He started down the tunnel, then turned to give her a parting shot. "See you on the dirt, *princess*."

Jessa stared after him, wishing the ground would open up and swallow her whole. It looked like Garrett wasn't the only one who would be apologizing today.

* * *

Strawberries.

You're such a dumbass.

What the hell was he thinking? If there was one thing every baseball player knew, it was that you didn't fuck with the owner's daughter. Ever.

And there he was ... talking goddamned condoms and telling her she'd made him hungry.

Jesus Christ.

Garrett scrubbed his hand down his face. He'd heard about the beautiful Jessa Montgomery. From what he'd seen just now, she'd earned every ounce of praise. She was a total knockout. Her hair was a gorgeous shade of blonde and copper, long enough to drape over her breasts. Breasts that weren't overly large, but perfect to fill his hands.

And her eyes. Garrett bit back a moan. Her eyes were mesmerizing. Not quite blue, not quite green.

But when she started rattling off stats with that voice as smooth as honey, sweet mercy, he'd gone rock hard. Which was damned uncomfortable when his junk was crammed into a protective cup.

Not even his mother could rattle off stats like that and know what they meant. The fact that Jessa understood the game he loved? Fucking. Sexy.

Garrett reached down to adjust himself, hoping to get some relief from the pinch currently nagging his balls.

Two weeks. He'd better chill the fuck out if he was going to survive two weeks with Jessa. Garrett respected the hell out of TJ Montgomery. It was rare for TJ to take a personal interest to the extent he had with him. He still hadn't figured that one out, but Garrett liked the man. And he needed this job. He had his mom and

Leah to worry about. And now little Georgia Grace.

His dad had died years ago, and now that his brother-in-law was gone, Garrett was all they had. The family farm in Mississippi had been his parents' dream, and Garrett worked hard to make sure it would continue to provide for them. But there was only so much he could do by himself.

Baseball was his ticket to securing a future for his family. He couldn't afford to screw that up. He had no business thinking about strawberries and wondering if Jessa's nipples would taste the same as she smelled.

Shit.

Garrett made his way onto the field. He didn't know what she was getting all bent out of shape about anyway. Even being a few hours later than he'd scheduled, he was still two days early for team practice. If anything, *he* should be offended about the crack she'd made about him wearing protection. As if he was some kind of man whore.

Ah, if only he'd had that kind of time to waste.

He scanned the growing crowd. He smiled and waved to the fans calling his name. He took in the excitement like the ground soaked up the sun, giving himself a moment to revel in the fact that he was here. All the years of hard work and sacrifice had finally paid off.

"Hey, Donovan!" Garrett turned to see the batting coach signaling him over. "You planning to stand around all day, or you gonna show these folks whatcha got?"

He caught sight of Jessa, already sitting in the first row with her bare feet propped up on the rail. He couldn't resist stretching his neck to check out her long, lean legs. He cursed as she eased out of the short-sleeved button down, leaving her in a tight top with tiny straps. He wondered how easily those straps would snap if he wrapped his hands around them and tugged.

As if she sensed him watching, her gaze locked on him. Her smile was almost apologetic. Then she laughed and waved her clipboard — her demand for him to get busy.

"Donovan!"

Garrett grabbed his bat and sighed. It was going to be a very long two weeks.

CHAPTER TWO

Jessa had always prided herself on self-control. She'd need every ounce if she was going to survive the next couple of weeks.

There was no denying her attraction to Garrett. Her body had lit up like an amusement park the second she'd laid eyes on him. As though it recognized him as the one who could show it indescribable pleasure. Her experience with men may have been limited, but she was far from innocent. Yet, ten minutes with Garrett Donovan and she was a hot mess. The reaction surprised her, set her on edge.

She dropped her purse and keycard on the table and went straight for the shower. She stripped off her clothes, leaving them scattered across the floor. She stepped into the glass enclosure and yelped, her back arching as the cold water hit her skin. Tiny bumps erupted across her body and her nipples drew up tight. After a quick readjust, lukewarm water flowed. Just enough to take the edge off.

She hoped.

Smoothing her hands down her body, Jessa let out a soft moan as she washed away the sweat and grime of the ballpark. She'd had worse days. Even if Garrett hadn't been so yummy to look at, his talent as an athlete was truly a sight to behold. His confidence lacked the arrogance she was used to. He moved with fluid grace, comfortable in his own skin. And when he'd stopped to sign autographs and talk to the fans, his smile was one of genuine happiness.

She'd never seen anything like it.

Her eyes drifted closed and she saw him. The way his hands stroked over his bat as he stepped into the box. The way his tongue wet his bottom lip as he twisted his foot and dug in.

Palming her breasts, Jessa thumbed the tight buds, caressing the sensitive edges. How would his hands feel against her skin? Would he be gentle? Or rough and demanding?

Her womb tightened. Moisture flooded her sex. She imagined the smooth rotation of his hips as he swung, felt it as if he rode between her thighs. Her pelvis rocked forward, her pussy pulsating with need as her body took over her mind.

Jesus, she'd managed to turn batting practice into a porn flick.

Breathless and aroused, Jessa rested her forehead against the cool tile. She reached between her legs, pressing her fingers flat against the swollen lips of her pussy, knowing there wasn't much she could to do alleviate the tension. She'd rarely been able to get herself off with her fingers. To try would only result in further frustration and a serious hand cramp. Not the greatest time to have forgotten her vibrator, but how could she have known she'd need it?

She'd watched hours of footage of Garrett's game play. Of course she'd noticed he was a good-looking guy, but nothing could have prepared her for the sensual assault of his silky smooth voice, his wicked grin, his ... this was so not helping.

She held her breath and turned the handle all the way to cold. She jumped and giggled as the icy flow doused the heat building within her. Dancing on her toes, she stayed under as long as she could.

It didn't make any sense. She didn't even know Garrett. He'd made that painfully clear with his comment about why he was late. So why couldn't she stop thinking about him?

After towel drying her hair, Jessa dressed in her favorite worn-out T-shirt and shorts. Her suite had a bar — and not of the mini variety — but she chose a bottle of water from the refrigerator instead. She grabbed her laptop and settled on the couch to go over the day's results. If she was going to keep thinking about Garrett, it was best she keep it professional. She'd met her quota of cold showers for the day.

She'd finished going over the numbers when a soft knock sounded on her door. She glanced at her watch, surprised to see it was almost eight o'clock.

Her face heated when she glanced through the peephole to see Garrett — a pizza box in one hand and a six-pack dangling from the other. She took a step back. What the …?

Of course she'd have to see him eventually, but the memory of her shower and the wicked things she'd imagined were still fresh in her mind. And now he was here. In the flesh.

He knocked again.

She laid her forehead against the door and took a few steadying breaths. She could do this. He was her job, nothing more. She smoothed her hands over her hair and opened the door.

"You had dinner?" His lazy grin was infectious.

She shook her head. How could she turn him down when he looked at her like that? "I didn't realize how late it'd gotten." She stepped out of the way and motioned him in. He went straight for the bar and tossed the pizza on the counter.

"Nice suite. It got plates?" He pulled open door after door, searching the cabinets.

"Have a seat." She came around and nudged him out of the way, relieved at the lack of awkwardness between them. "What're you doing here, anyway?"

He shrugged. "Thought maybe we should start over. You know, get to know each other better."

"You think we're going to bond over pepperoni?"

"You know what they say. Nothing brings people together like a little Italian meat." He wagged his eyebrows.

"If you're about to say you're Italian, get out." She crooked a thumb at the door, but relaxed at his teasing.

"Not me, I'm just a small-town farm boy from Mississippi." He winked at her. "And I'm not little." He waggled his fingers at her. "See? Large hands," he teased.

Sweet Jesus, her imagination was active enough. Comments like that didn't help. "Right." She laughed and pulled two plates from the cabinet. She set one in front of him along with one of the beers he'd brought. She put the other cans in the fridge and took another bottle of water for herself.

He eyed her curiously. "You don't drink?" He helped himself to the pizza, tossing half the pie on his plate before he moved to the sofa.

She took two pieces and joined him. She settled in the corner, cross-legged with her plate resting on her lap. "Not really. I never got the point."

"You're what? Twenty-two?"

She rolled her eyes, darting her foot out to push at his leg. "Twenty-four. Same age as you."

"Right. Twenty-four." His gaze narrowed. "You a goodie-two-shoes or something?"

Jessa straightened her spine. She leaned over and wrapped her hand around his beer can. Keeping her gaze on his, she put the can to her lips and drank. The vile liquid made her shudder, but she didn't stop until the can was empty. She wrinkled her nose at him. "I didn't say I didn't drink. I said I don't see the point."

Garrett put a hand over his heart. "I think I'm in love."

She tossed the can at him — which he caught with a laugh — and she rose to get him another.

"Come on, you've never let loose? Let your hair down? Shook your moneymaker?" He made an obscene movement that made her jealous of the couch.

"If you mean do I go out and get drunk off my ass and act like an idiot ... then the answer is no. I prefer to keep a low profile, you know, for my dad."

Garrett nodded his head as if he understood and took a bite of pizza. "That's what TJ expects then?" he said around his food.

She handed him the beer. "Since you're on a first name basis, maybe you should ask him that question."

"Wow, touchy. Actually, I was wondering if your low profile was self-imposed or not." He trained his beautiful blues on her. "Before you go and get all huffy again, I'll tell you that I like your dad, Jessa. I'd say that's a good thing, considering he's my boss. And he's been good to me. Given me some great advice. Hell, he gave me a job. I'd say that puts him up there as one of my favorite people." He sank back into the sofa, resting his arm along the back and looking entirely too comfortable in her space.

She sat forward and put her plate on the coffee table. "I'm sorry. You're right, I am a bit sensitive about my dad." Although she had no idea why she was telling him about it.

"Any particular reason?"

She glanced at him over her shoulder. "Sometimes I'm painfully aware that I'm a girl. He's taken a liking to you in a way I've not seen him do before." She shrugged a shoulder. "Makes me think he wished for a son."

Garrett leaned forward. "Can I tell you a secret?" He motioned her closer. "I'm glad you're not a boy."

Jessa's heart thundered in her chest as his breath tickled her ear.

His warm, earthy aroma drifted to her nose. He smelled clean, like fresh cut grass after a spring rain. No cologne to mask his natural rich, male scent.

"Yes, well." She cleared her throat. "I've apparently misjudged you." She looked him in the eye. "I'm sorry for this morning, Garrett."

"Apology accepted. And?" he prompted.

She laughed, amazed at how he'd read her mind. She pushed at his shoulder, knocking him sideways on the couch "And, I'm sorry about that crack about my dad."

He laid back and folded his hands over his stomach. "For what it's worth, princess, I have no idea what I've done to deserve all his attention."

The sincerity in his expression surprised her, as did the moisture that seeped into her panties when he called her princess. "You're kidding, right?"

He remained silent.

"Garrett," she chastised. "You're the most promising shortstop to hit the club in, well, forever. You run like the wind, can hit practically anything thrown at you, and your glove is a mile wide." Truth was, if the Empire hadn't signed him, someone else would have. To say her dad gave him a job is a severe understatement. They were lucky to have him.

His cheeks reddened and he looked away from her. "Well, when you say it like that …" His voice was quiet. "Nothing wrong with being good at my job."

Oh, my God. She'd embarrassed him with his own talent. "From what I heard this morning, you also take care of your family." She turned to study him as a thought occurred. "You've been taking care of them for a long time, haven't you?"

"All my life." He muttered so soft she almost missed it. Then louder, "It's just my mom, my sister, Leah, and me."

"And your niece?"

He seemed surprised she'd remembered. "Yeah." He exaggerated a sigh. "Georgia Grace. Another girl."

He wasn't fooling her. His eyes had shone with love the minute she'd mentioned his niece. Jessa's heart melted. "I think I just figured out why my dad likes you so much."

His expression turned serious, intense. "Does that mean you're starting to like me?"

She winked at him, ignoring the flutter in her stomach. "Maybe a little."

He reached out and cupped her face, stroking his thumb across her cheek. "Just a little?"

She stared back at him, struggling to breathe. She trembled, turned into his touch, and rubbed her cheek against his palm.

"I really want to kiss you right now," he whispered.

She drew a breath as desire coursed through her veins. She licked her lips in anticipation, her voice nothing more than a mere sigh. "I won't stop you."

CHAPTER THREE

"Jessa." Garrett's eyes sparked as he leaned in. His lips fondled hers, the contact light, gentle. Sweet. Too sweet.

Not enough.

His tongue grazed her lips and she parted, eager to draw him inside her mouth when he seemed content to stay out. He lazily supped at her lips, tracing every line and ridge. He nibbled and tasted, teased her with the promise of more, but denied her the deeper touch her body yearned for.

She broke the contact. She swung a leg over to straddle him and rested her palms against his chest. His eyes darkened with lust as he moved his hips under her, settling her tight against him. His hands curved around and gripped her ass. His heart beat heavy under her palms, driving her own need higher with every thump.

"What are we doing?" she wondered aloud.

His smile was slow, seductive. "Kissing." He wrapped a hand in her hair and brought her mouth back to his. This time, he didn't tease her. The moment their lips touched, his tongue pushed inside and his taste exploded in her mouth. The subtle hint of beer mingled with the unique flavor that she instinctively knew was all Garrett.

She speared her hands into the soft waves of his hair and held him to her. She pressed her chest against him as she stroked his tongue with hers. A moan tore from her throat as his hands moved to her hips and held fast.

"Sit still," he whispered against her lips. "Let me enjoy that beautiful mouth of yours for a bit."

Heat infused her cheeks as she realized she'd been rocking against him, driven by her need to feel more. And he wasn't unaffected, if the erection pushing against her was any indication.

"Aw, now, look at that." He brushed his lips over her cheek, down the side of her jaw. "You blush a lot. You're so pretty when you blush. Do I make you nervous?"

She shuddered a breath. Hot, wet, horny. Nervous? No. "You make me …"

"What? What do I make you, baby?"

She snickered. "Needy."

His laugh rumbled against her neck and she tilted her head to give him better access, letting her hands rest on his shoulders. She forced her hips to remain still as he laved at her neck, curled his tongue around her earlobe, trailed to the sensitive flesh behind. She whimpered, sliding her fingers to cup his neck, needing to feel his skin against hers however she could get it.

Arousal, hot and hard, fired in her blood. Perspiration formed on her skin as she fought the need clawing at her belly.

He shifted, his cock pressing against her aching clit until she couldn't take anymore. She had never wanted anything as much as she wanted him right now. "Garrett, please. Touch me."

His mouth never left her neck as he held her, turned, and laid her under him. She loved the feel of his weight on her, his hard curves and angles pressing into her most intimate places. She wrapped her legs around his waist, cradling him between her thighs.

Hunger burned in his eyes, his expression pained. "Jesus, Jessa. You're going to kill me." His mouth was already moving, burning a trail across her throat. He eased to one side, his hand catching the hem of her shirt, lifting it to reveal her belly. Her vagina contracted, releasing proof of her arousal, dampening her already moist panties.

Her breath caught as he feathered his fingertips across her skin. They should stop. Her dad would kill them both if he ever found out, and Garrett had much more to lose than she did. Her dad would forgive her for messing around with one of his players. But Garrett, his penalty could be much more severe.

"Don't ever get involved, Jessa." Her dad's warning echoed through

her head. How many times had he uttered that sentence? A hundred? A thousand? She'd never been tempted before.

She was tempted now.

She didn't think her dad would go so far as to fire him. Truth was, she didn't know what he'd do. At the very least, Garrett's reputation could be tarnished.

His distracting fingers grazed the edge of her breast, almost depleting her reserve of self-control. "Wait." She locked her hand around his wrist. "We have to stop."

Awareness dawned in his eyes. He drew an unsteady breath as he rested his forehead against hers. "Oh, fuck. Jessa. I'm sorry. I don't know what ... *fuck*." He rolled off her and fell to the floor.

She was relieved to see he was as lost as she was. She turned, propped her head in her hand, and gazed down at him. God, he was gorgeous. His hair was cut shorter than she'd seen before, but was still long enough to appear mussed from her fingers. His lips were drawn tight, the muscles in his cheeks working overtime. The impressive bulge in his jeans made her mouth water. She forced her gaze away, dangerously close to forgetting why she'd stopped.

She soothed a finger over his forehead. "You're going to break your teeth."

He kept his eyes closed. "Gimme a minute and I'll head out."

"No rush."

His eyes snapped open. Pure, animal lust burned in a sea of blue. "You sure about that? Because right now all I can think of is how good your mouth tastes and how hot your pussy felt rubbing against me. I want nothing more than to fuck the shit out of you right now, Jessa." He grimaced. "Still think I should hang around?"

Yes, please! She groaned and rolled to her back, his brutal words making her quiver at the possibility. "Do you have to be so crude about it?" So primal.

He pushed to his feet. "I'm not being crude. I'm being honest." He shoved his hands through his hair, lacing them together behind his neck. "I could give you flowery words, all pretty and delicate. Hell, you deserve that." He pinned her with a stare. "But I'm not feeling all that delicate right now. My gut is burning with the need to bend you over that table and ..." His voice turned guttural. "Time to go."

Jessa sat up with the intent to follow, but he stopped her with a look. "Keep your seat, I can see myself out."

She sat back and brought her knees to her chest. "Garrett?" Don't go. She didn't know what else to say. "Thanks for the pizza."

He chuckled as he opened the door, waving a hand to let her know he'd heard her. "You betcha."

* * *

He was in trouble. Garrett stared at the ceiling and grit his teeth against the lust that ravaged his body. His little stunt in Jessa's room had changed everything. Started a firestorm in his system that only one thing would extinguish. The one thing he couldn't let happen.

Christ, what the fuck was he thinking?

He grabbed another ball from the bag at his feet. He was going to get himself traded. Then what? He could play for another team, but his reputation would be ruined. He'd be known as *that guy* for the rest of his career. Shit like that didn't just blow over.

He scrawled his name across the ball before tossing it into the basket beside him. His hand was cramped and he'd barely made a dent in the bag. At the rate he was going, he'd be up all night.

In more ways than one.

He'd gone over and over it in his head. He hadn't intended to take advantage of Jessa. He'd wanted to make peace with her, start over fresh. Kissing her had been an impulse, but one he couldn't have stopped if he'd tried. Her lips, curled into that gentle smile as she teased him, were far too much temptation for a mortal man such as himself.

Once he'd tasted her, the only thing on his mind was *more*. More heat, more skin, more Jessa.

What was it about her that made him forget everything else?

He'd spent years honing his instinct. Hell, it's what made him the ballplayer he was today. He could see the play in his head before the bat hit the ball. He didn't question it. He rolled with it, did whatever it took to get the job done.

His father's voice echoed in his head. Work hard. Take care of your own. Trust your gut.

Right now, Garrett's gut was doing the mambo.

He signed another ball and added it to the growing pile. He was here to play baseball, not to get laid. His cock jerked in protest as the vision of Jessa, spread out beneath him, filled his head.

"Damn it." His curse broke through the silence of the room. He went to the bar to grab a beer, only to realize he'd left them in Jessa's fridge. Whiskey then. Just a shot. Not enough to make him sorry tomorrow, but enough to help him avoid the horror of a cold shower.

He carried the tumbler back to the couch, clicked on the TV and resumed signing the baseballs his agent had sent over. He scribed ball after ball, half listening to the sports recap on the TV and more thinking about Jessa. He tossed the marker on the table and finished his drink.

Before he realized what he was doing, he slipped his hand into his shorts and wrapped it around his swollen length. His head fell to the back of the couch. Using his other hand, he pulled the elastic waistband down and hooked it around his balls. His breath caught at the added pressure to the sensitive area behind his testicles.

He worked his fist over his cock, circling the base and moving upward, squeezing the tip until moisture beaded from the head. His hips jerked as he spread the warm fluid around with this thumb before moving to the base to begin again.

Jessa's taste was still in his mouth. She tasted fresh, sweet. Her tongue an eager partner in the dance he'd started.

He raised his head and watched as he stroked himself. His cock throbbed, as if angry the only heat it felt was from his own hand.

Jessa would be in bed now, sheets caressing her naked flesh. Oh yeah, she'd be naked. And touching herself as he was. Nimble fingers tugging at her tight little nipples. Would she pull hard, or roll them gently between her fingers? Would she need the added twinge to bring her greater pleasure? He was dying to find out.

Sweat beaded on his upper lip as he tightened his grip. The thought of her stretched out and open, her pussy wet with need, made him desperate to come. He imagined her delicate folds bare, nothing between him and the sensitive nerve endings that would come alive with his touch. He'd take her slow, learning what made his little kitten purr. Swiping his tongue through her slit, he'd draw her essence into him, letting it soothe his throat until he was drunk on her. He'd suck her outer folds into his mouth, first one, then the other. Nibbling at the tender skin until she cried his name. He'd use his fingers to spread her open, memorizing her beautiful shape, before plunging his tongue deep inside, teasing, driving her to the edge of orgasm. But he'd not let her over the edge. Not yet.

She'd grab his head, holding him in place as she rode his tongue, begging him to give her what she craved.

He'd make her crazy with need.

As crazy as he was as he pumped his cock harder, faster. Sweat ran down his chest. He reached with his free hand and grabbed his sac. His heart hammered in his ears, his breath caught as his thighs and stomach tightened. Further thought became impossible. Jessa's image was all he could hold on to as his release hit him. His breath held, his hips lifted from the couch as his seed spilled across his stomach and chest.

Reality was slow to return. His panting breath and the ringing in his ears the only sounds he could hear. This wasn't the first time he'd masturbated, but shit. He'd never felt anything like that before. If his release was that intense just thinking about Jessa, then actually being inside her would kill him for sure.

Two weeks. He licked his lips and grinned at the thought. He knew the dangers of messing with her. If he was smart, he'd leave her the hell alone. Maybe he would have, if she hadn't come alive in his arms tonight. If she hadn't returned his kiss with fiery passion, if she hadn't begged him to touch her as she cushioned his hips with her own.

Nope, he wasn't smart at all. Dumb as a fuckin' post, in fact, because he knew there was no way he could leave her alone. His cock twitched. He grimaced as his fingers touched the sticky fluid on his stomach.

Fuck.

Seems he was gonna get that cold shower after all.

CHAPTER FOUR

Jessa nursed her hot tea while she waited for Garrett to join her in the limo. She was filled with nervous energy, not knowing what to expect this morning. She'd spent half the night aroused and the other half worried about where things stood between them. They'd hardly been intimate, but they'd done enough to cause problems with their working relationship if they weren't careful.

A kiss. God, one kiss and she'd been lost. She'd never begged anyone to touch her, but last night with Garrett, it was the only thing she could do. He'd stolen her need for anything but his next touch. The things she'd said, the things she'd done …

And now she had to face him.

Good lord.

She palmed her flaming cheeks, feeling like a silly teenager with her first crush.

They had to talk about what happened, because it couldn't happen again. Her dad would freak the hell out. She wouldn't risk Garrett's job that way, no matter how badly she wanted him.

And speak of the devil. Garrett jerked opened the door and she suppressed a laugh as he all but fell inside. He tossed a canvas bag on the floor, several baseballs falling out and rolling around her feet. He passed her a heated glance and slid onto the seat next to her.

"Nice digs," he grumbled. "Though I'd much rather have a regular old car. I hear they rent those nowadays."

"Let me guess." She scooted to the side, his grumpy mood setting her further on edge. "Not a morning person?"

He turned his head toward her, his eyes narrowing. "I didn't sleep well. Stayed up signing baseballs. Then ... well, let's just say it was a restless night. Normally, I'd forgo caffeine during training, but I'd kill for a cup of coffee right about now." He eyed her travel mug for a second before reaching over, snatching it from her and taking a drink. Tiny droplets spewed from his lips, misting over the floor and seat across from them. "Ah, damn! What the hell is this shit?" His face scrunched up as he wiped the back of his hand across his mouth.

"It's green tea. Very good for you."

Garrett gave her mug a dirty look before passing it back. "I don't care how good it is for me, that shit is nasty."

"Big baby," she teased, and produced a large cup of coffee she'd gotten from the hotel. "I thought you might need this."

His face lit up and stole her breath. He slid close, taking the cup out of her hands. His eyes gleamed and he held the cup as if she'd given him something precious and fragile. "There is a God, and she's the prettiest thing I've ever seen." He took a drink and sighed. "Thank you, darlin'." His head fell back and he closed his eyes.

"You're welcome, sweetie pie." She did her best to mimic his accent.

He cracked one eye open. "Cheeky."

Jessa studied him, wishing she knew him well enough to understand his moods. His eyes were closed, his face relaxed. She studied the contours of his face, the stubble on his cheeks and chin giving him a rugged look. He raised the cup to his mouth and she watched, fascinated, as his lips pursed to blow over the hot brew. His tongue darted out to lick the edge of the lid before he sipped, all the while keeping his eyes shut and his head tilted back. God, only Garrett could make drinking coffee sexy.

"You know, it's impolite to stare." His lips curled up, but otherwise he remained still. "But, I'll tell you what." He moved then, setting his coffee aside and patting his lap. "Climb on up and stare all you want."

"Be serious." He had no idea how much she wanted to take him up on his offer.

"Oh, I am serious." He patted his lap again. "Come on, princess. You know you want to. If you're gonna make me ride to the park in this God-forsaken vehicle, then I need some perks." He eyed her breasts and her traitorous nipples jumped for joy.

"The limo's not a perk?"

"Hardly."

"Well, then that coffee's the only perk you're getting this morning, so you better enjoy it while it's hot."

He grumbled again, but grabbed his cup and resumed his position.

"Garrett, we need to talk about last night." Butterflies erupted in her stomach as she broached the subject.

"Sit on my lap and we'll talk."

The roughness of his voice sent a shiver up her spine. The sensation branched out, coursed through her veins as if he'd touched her.

"You're not helping."

"I didn't know I was supposed to be."

She threw her hands up. "Jesus, you're impossible!"

His expression was one of pure male irritation. "Fine. Talk." He cocked a brow as he waited for her to say something.

She scowled. She hadn't slept well either, but she wasn't taking it out on him. "You don't have to be so testy."

"I'm running on no sleep and very little coffee. I'm gonna get shit like you won't believe for showing up in this fancy rig every day when a fucking rental car would have suited me just fine." He blew out a breath and ran his hand over his head. "Now, you're about to give me all the reasons why last night was a mistake. You'll rationalize, throw my job and your father at me. Then, you'll tell me it can't ever happen again. I'd be surprised if you didn't try to give me the 'let's be friends' bit. I get it. Hell, I'll probably even agree with you." His eyes turned dark, his voice strained. "And then you'll expect me to forget how you burned in my arms and that I'm so hard for you right now I can't see straight. So, yeah, Jessa. I'm a little fuckin' testy."

Stunned, Jessa bit her cheek. Her gaze darted to his lap, eliciting a growl from him as he shifted to the seat across from her. The move poked at her temper. "You know, you aren't the only one who had a rough night so you can shove the attitude. You can have a *fucking rental car* after I leave. The limo wasn't my idea. Dad insisted." Tears threatened the edges of her lids and Jessa rolled her head back in an effort to keep them from trailing down her cheeks. Garrett had been right, about most of it anyway. Deep down, she knew he wasn't mad at her. It wasn't her fault, hell, it wasn't anyone's fault. Things were how they were and that meant it sucked to be them right now.

"Great. Talk over?"

She turned to the window. "I guess that pretty much covers it. I wish ..." She didn't know what she wished. That he played for a different team? That her dad wouldn't have a coronary at the thought of her dating a ballplayer — one of *his* ballplayers? That the sight of Garrett didn't make her weak?

Yeah, that about covered it.

He cursed and sat forward, his arms braced on his knees. "Jesus, Jess. I'm sorry. I'm a total bastard without sleep. I didn't mean to attack you like that."

She nodded. "You were wrong about one thing."

He raised a questioning brow.

"I wasn't going to tell you last night was a mistake."

He seemed to consider her words before he sunk back into the seat. "That's good, because I'm not sorry about last night either. So, that leaves us ... where exactly?"

She cringed at what was about to come out of her mouth. "As friends, I guess? We both have jobs to do, and at the end of next week I'll be back in New York and you'll be in the thick of pre-season games. It's better if we stay focused on what we're here to do. But, you're right." She smirked and blinked her eyelashes at him. "You are a total bastard."

Garrett barked a laugh, the sound ringing her ears as the tension around them lessened. "Now that we have that cleared up, some of the guys and their wives are going out to dinner tonight. You wanna go?"

Her heart skipped a beat. "Like a date?" Hadn't they just been over this?

"Nope. Like dinner. *Friends,* remember?"

She shook her head. "I don't think so."

"Why not?"

The playful spark in his eyes made her grateful his mood seemed to be improving. She hoped it lasted. "No."

"I thought you were supposed to keep an eye on me." He gave her that smile again. The one that promised long, slow, deep pleasure.

Damn him.

"Oh, that's right, Jessa. I know all about why you're here. So, what's to stop me from doing something stupid if you aren't there to make sure I behave myself?"

Jessa knew what he was doing. Using that wicked Southern

charm to goad her into going. "I have responsibilities, Garrett." She leveled her gaze on him. "I can't go out drinking with a bunch of ballplayers."

"And their wives," he added. "For dinner. If you don't want to drink, don't drink. Eat, dance, laugh. Blow off steam like the rest of us. Besides, I'm one of your responsibilities. And I'm going out tonight. Sure would be nice to have a chaperone." His sing-songy voice trailed off as he watched her.

"It's weird for me," she blurted. She hated to admit it, but she wanted him to understand.

"Dinner is weird?"

"Jesus, Garrett." She laughed, amazed at the difference a few ounces of caffeine could make. "No. People are different around me, you know, because of my dad. It's really hard to get to know someone when they're always afraid to speak their minds for fear I'll run and tell him every word. I don't want to spend the evening with a bunch of people being fake nice to me."

He put a hand over his heart. "I give you my word it won't be like that. Come on, Jess. Live a little. You *do* know how to have fun, don't you?"

The challenge was clear. She pinched the bridge of her nose. It was too early to have a headache but she was fast on her way. Her dad had accused her of never having any fun, and now Garrett. Well, to hell with both of them. She could have fun. And she'd go all out, too. Hair, makeup, new outfit. The works. Which meant she'd have to get busy.

"All right, Garrett."

His smile morphed into a frown. "What is that look? And why am I suddenly scared?"

She reached over and patted him on the knee. "It'll be okay. You're right. I'll go. It's about time I stepped out."

* * *

Jessa cocked her head to the side and stared at the woman in the mirror as if she were a complete stranger.

I can't do this.

She'd managed to get a little work done that morning, but with Garrett spending the majority of the day with his strength coach and working the PR schedule his agent had set up, she hadn't felt too guilty about slipping out early.

She'd spent the first two hours at a local spa she'd found that could work her in. She'd walked out waxed and buffed and feeling more relaxed than she had in days.

Until the shopping.

Jessa hated shopping. She didn't consider herself a tomboy. She wore makeup — okay, maybe not on a regular basis, but still. She highlighted her hair and enjoyed getting her fingers and toes painted. That was where her girly-ness ended. She was way more comfortable barefoot, wearing jeans and a T-shirt than in one of the fancy dresses that were stored in the back of her closet. She rarely dressed up for work either, since she did most of her stuff remotely, whether from a sky box, a hotel room, or the home she still shared with her dad.

Jessa didn't know much about fashion, and didn't really care. Another thing that made her weird to the women she'd tried to develop friendships with over the years. To save herself time and frustration, she'd walked into a fancy department store, found the nearest sales person who looked about her age, and gave herself over.

Now she had another dress for her collection. She chewed on her bottom lip, her stomach flipping end over end.

The salesgirl had sworn the dress was perfect for dinner. It wasn't the dress that made Jessa nervous; it was the lack of it that gave her pause.

She studied her reflection. The shimmering, black halter dress glittered as she swayed her hips from side to side. The plunging neckline accentuated her breasts, the material forcing them into cleavage she'd never have otherwise. The fabric was snug along her trim waist, only to flair out into a flowing skirt that ended right below her knees. Sexy, yet not over the top.

She'd balked at the salesgirl's suggestion for new lingerie. It's not like she could wear a bra, since the dress was open to the curve of her lower back. But the girl insisted and Jessa had to admit it was a rush — the thigh-highs and garter a secret only she knew.

Jessa leaned in and reapplied a light pink gloss to her lips. The woman who'd done her hair also happened to do makeup — lucky her — so she'd willingly let others put on her armor for the evening. And the truth was, she felt pretty. Not something she usually worried about much, but as she smoothed her hands over the shining ringlets that tumbled over her shoulders, she wondered how she'd appear through Garrett's eyes.

Not that she cared. She didn't. Nope.

A knock on her door startled her out of her musings.

It wasn't too late to back out. She could throw on some shorts and a T-shirt and curl up with a movie.

No. She wasn't a coward. Garrett hadn't told her who was joining them, but he'd assured her everything would be fine. And even if it wasn't, she'd been down this road thousands of times. It came with the territory when you had a father who was not only rich, but famous as well.

She grabbed the tiny purse that held her essentials, pasted a smile on her face, and jerked open the door.

Garrett's eyes went wide at the sight of her. His gaze made a slow descent from her face to her feet, then — with the same agonizing pace — headed back up. She stood still, forcing herself not to fidget as he took her in.

Her hand shook as she placed it in the one he offered and he eased her into the hallway.

"Holy shit." Garrett whistled as he spun her around.

Jessa laughed, pleased with his reaction. "Such the Southern gentleman." She bobbed a curtsy. "You like it?"

His eyes turned dark and her chest constricted. "Princess, that dress is gonna make me forget my manners."

She raised her chin. "I'm going to take that as a compliment."

"Uh-huh."

"Garrett?" A thrill of excitement shot through her as his tongue swept across his lips. It was wrong to delight in his reaction, but she couldn't keep the smile from her face. "We don't want to be late."

CHAPTER FIVE

The restaurant was crowded, but not packed like she'd expected. She'd never been here before, but, at first glance, Jessa knew it was her kind of place.

Comfortable-looking leather chairs accompanied mosaic tabletops in rich, warm colors. Exposed beams were stained dark, and candles lit every table, giving off an intimate, romantic feel. A huge brick oven and open fire grill took up an entire wall. The delicious array of aromas made her mouth water.

Soft sounds drifted from an area where people were dancing. Not the bump and grind one would expect in Tampa, but a more classic style that complemented the smooth, Sinatra-esque music playing. Jessa was instantly enchanted.

Her three-inch heels clicked against the mismatched stone floor and she prayed she wouldn't fall and break her neck. The pretty hostess fawned over Garrett, casting flirty glances over her shoulder as she escorted them to their table. Garrett was all smiles, chatting with her about her favorite food and drink selections. The girl acted as if she might actually swoon at the attention.

When they arrived at their table, Garrett took the girl's hand and brought her knuckles to his lips. "Thank you for the assist." When he winked, Jessa saw he'd placed a bill in her palm. It was sweet of him to tip the girl, but did he have to be so blasted charming about it?

Jessa leaned over and kept her voice low. "You slip her your room number, too?"

Garrett looked at her as if she'd grown horns. "You kidding? She's a baby for chrissake. I'm not going to jail over a piece of ass." He shook his head. "I can't believe you asked me that."

Jessa shrugged him off and turned to greet the others at the table. Jim was there, along with his wife, Joanna. Jim's constant sidekick and catcher Miles Sturdivant sat next to them with his wife, Amy. Renowned bad boy and first baseman Tyler Brady, who was also one of Garrett's closest friends from college if she remembered correctly, rounded out the group.

Jim stood and reached for her hand. "Jessa, it's nice to see you. I was surprised when Garrett said you'd be joining us tonight. You remember my wife, Joanna?"

"Of course." Jessa shook Jim's hand. "It's lovely to see you both again." She extended her hand to Miles, then Amy. "It's good to see you, Miles. Amy." She smiled at the men and fidgeted with the strap on her purse. "You guys are looking good out there."

Well, this isn't awkward.

Garrett signaled to the waiter and pointed Jessa toward an empty chair.

"What about me, pretty girl?" Tyler stood, making Jessa crane her neck.

Tyler's smile was so beautiful it made her teeth hurt. It was easy to see why women fell at his feet. His hair was longer and a shade lighter than Garrett's, but they had the same piercing blue eyes. Growing up in neighboring states, Tyler even had the same smooth, Southern lilt that Garrett sported. Hell, they could've been brothers.

Tyler was way too handsome for his own good. Good thing she was immune. There was only one man here tonight who made her pulse race.

Tyler took her hand and pulled her close. "Nice dress."

Garrett made a noise as Jessa pushed at Tyler's chest. "Uh, thanks, Tyler. Nice to see you, too. Now, get off me." She laughed nervously, giving him a shove. She'd known him for a few years, but he'd never tried to hug her before. She had no idea what had prompted the display now.

Tyler released her, laughing so loud several people turned to stare. "So, Jessa Montgomery," he drawled. "Out with the little people, huh? You decide to do a little slummin' tonight?"

Garrett stiffened at her side. "Damn it, Tyler."

Jessa gripped Garrett's forearm as he tried to step in front of her. She glanced around the table. Wide eyes were on her, as if waiting for her reaction. She turned to Tyler again, his eyes gleamed with amusement. Testing her, was he? Setting the tone for the evening? She didn't know whether to be grateful or to kick his arrogant ass.

"You know," she tapped her chin with her finger, "that thought never crossed my mind." She tilted her head and considered him. "Until I saw *you*, that is." She put her hand to the side of her mouth and whispered to Garrett, loud enough for everyone to hear. "Tyler definitely qualifies as slummin', don't you think?"

Garrett laughed and gave Tyler a smug smile. "You got my vote on that one, darlin'."

"Mine, too." Miles chimed in.

"Hear, hear!" Jim pounded his fist on the table.

"Any girl that can call Tyler on his bullshit is a girl I want to know. Here, Jessa." Joanna had the guys move around until the chair next to her was empty. "Sit. Let the boys have their beer and whiskey and talk shop while us girls get better acquainted. Amy and I have decided to make our way through the list of girly, fruity drinks. What's next on the list, Ames?"

Amy's smile was so sincere, Jessa almost cringed. God, she was such a bitch for expecting the worst from them. If she didn't want to be judged, then she needed to stop judging. She returned Amy's smile, promising herself then and there that she'd do better.

"Something called a Bellini. It's got champagne in it. You game, Jessa?"

Jessa glanced to see Garrett already had a beer in hand and was in some sort of heated discussion with Tyler. "Sure, count me in. I'll have a couple with you." She'd hold fast to her two-drink rule. Three tops.

Joanna placed their drink order and turned back to discuss dinner options. Her shoulder length chestnut hair swayed as she talked, her hazel eyes sharp. Jessa would bet there wasn't much that got past her. She wore a dark blue sundress that showed off her ample cleavage and toned arms, making Jessa wonder if she spent as much time in the gym as she did.

Amy, on the other hand, was stunning with her bright red hair, blue eyes and pale skin. Her yellow halter and short skirt made Jessa feel much better about her own wardrobe choice. And Amy liked to talk with her hands when she got excited. Apparently, the prime rib was definitely wave-worthy so Jessa decided to trust Amy's choice and ordered that, along with a salad and another drink. A Cosmo was next, because, Amy had explained, the menu listed the drinks in alphabetical order.

Once their orders were taken and drinks delivered, Joanna clapped her hands together and turned her full attention on Jessa. "So, what brings you to spring training this year, Jessa? I've never known you to hang out in the trenches this time of year."

"Dad sent me." She jutted her chin toward Garrett. "To keep an eye on golden boy over there." Her heart fluttered. He was so handsome in his black slacks and dress shirt, paired with a gray sport coat.

Joanna and Amy shared a look, then stared at Garrett.

Jessa turned back to Garrett and judging by the scowl on his face, he'd heard her 'golden boy' comment. Too bad. Not like she hadn't said it before. She faced the women again. "What did I miss?"

"He's never done that before? Your dad, I mean." Amy asked.

Jessa sipped her drink, enjoying the warmth that infused her belly. "Hmm. Nope, first time. That's weird, right?"

One would think she'd have attended at least one spring training by now, so the fact that this was her first seemed very odd indeed.

The ladies shared another glance that had Jessa gritting her teeth. She was definitely missing something.

They were interrupted by salads and Joanna rearranged them again, putting her between Garrett and Tyler. Jeez, Jessa hoped she could eat surrounded by all that testosterone.

As it turned out, she could. The prime rib had been as delicious as Amy had promised, the conversation flowed easily, and Jessa relaxed, feeling at ease in their company. Even Tyler, who was attentive and flirty, made her feel comfortable and welcome in their little group.

Garrett, she'd noticed, hadn't said much once they'd settled in to eat and she'd asked him more than once if he'd been feeling well. She got grunts and nods of affirmation, but not much else so she'd given up trying to talk to him.

After she finished her second drink, it was her turn to order up the next round. She consulted the menu. "What's next on the list?"

"Dances with Wenches!" Amy looked around the table in obvious glee. "Get ready boys, cause *we're* the wenches and *you're* going to dance with us!"

And just like that, Jessa found herself part of the club. "What the heck is a Dances with Wenches?" She wasn't drinking anything without knowing what was in it. With her luck, it'd be some homebrew mead or something equally gross.

Amy waved her off. "It's got cranberry juice in it, so it can't be all bad. Live a little!"

Jessa was sick and tired of people saying that to her.

Joanna tugged at Jim's hand. "Come on, husband. Dance with your wench." Jim laughed as he spun her away, followed closely by Miles and Amy.

Tyler stood and extended a hand to her. "Well, how about it, pretty girl? You up for a spin?"

Jessa glanced at Garrett. His scowl was starting to piss her off. This whole evening had been his idea. She pushed her chair back and put her hand in Tyler's. "Let's do it."

* * *

Garrett was going to kill his friend. Right here. In front of witnesses.

Dinner was not going at all like he'd planned. Of course, his expectations had been blown to shit this morning in the limo, so the fact that he'd planned anything was ridiculous. But he had, and not once did it include Tyler-fucking-Brady's hands all over Jessa's back as they danced. Her bare back. Nor did his plan include Tyler whispering something in her ear that caused her to throw her head back with laughter, exposing the sleek line of her neck, and God knew what else, to Tyler's gaze.

Jesus fucking Christ. There was only so much a man could take. He pushed away from the table. If Jessa was going to dance, she'd damn well do it with him.

He propped himself against a beam close to the dance floor and waited. He wasted no time making his move once the song came to an end. "My turn." He extended his hand. Jessa's cheeks were flushed a pretty pink and it was all he could do not to kiss her right then and there.

Garrett bristled as Tyler brought Jessa's knuckles to his lips. "Thanks for the dance, pretty girl. I enjoyed every minute of it."

Jessa's laugh was one of pure delight, which only added to Garrett's irritation. "Oh, no, the pleasure was all mine. Thank you," she cooed. She clutched her fists over her chest. "I don't remember when I've had so much fun! You're a great dancer, Tyler."

Tyler winked at her. "Save me another?"

Jessa nodded. "Absolutely!"

Garrett pulled her into his arms, turning her away from Tyler. The music was slow and Garrett was grateful for it. "Aren't you supposed to be watching me?" He couldn't stop himself. He was being a total dick, and yet, with the image of Tyler's hands on her still fresh in his mind, he couldn't seem to care.

Jessa gave him a wary look. "Why, are you about to do something stupid?"

Very, very stupid, according to the size of his erection. "You know, Tyler only wants one thing from you, princess."

The minute the words left his mouth, he'd regretted them. His own thoughts about Jessa over the last twenty-four hours weren't exactly pure and innocent either. Oh no, his thoughts had been more of the naked and wet variety.

So, what would be his claim? That he'd seen her first? Wanting Jessa in his bed, knowing it would be nothing more than a night or two, didn't make him any better than Tyler for the one-nighters he enjoyed.

Garrett needed to face the facts. A few days from now she'd be on the way back to New York and he'd have a season to play out.

He should walk away from her right now.

Yeah. Not fucking likely.

"People always want something from me," she murmured. "But, this ought to be good. Please, do tell."

"Jessa," he warned. "I've known Tyler a long time. Love him like a brother." *Except when he has his hands on you.* "But, he's not the kind of guy that sticks around, if you know what I mean."

She pulled back. "Are you jealous?"

"Of Tyler?"

"You sound a little jealous." She wasn't even trying to hide her amusement.

He bent to her ear, letting the warmth of his breath caress her. "And if I am?"

Her skin erupted in goose bumps and her breath hitched. "Don't do that."

"Do what?" He pressed his cheek against her hair, enjoying the silky feel of her curls against his skin. Curls he was dying to fist as she sucked him into the heaven that was her mouth.

She jerked her head away. "Stop it, Garrett."

She wiggled, moving her arm until it hooked his, successfully removing his palm from the heat of her skin. She grabbed his wrist and brought his hand to the back of her neck. "Keep your hand there."

Oh, so Tyler could touch her, but he couldn't?

He tightened his grip on the hand he held. "Something about my touch bother you, princess? You didn't have a problem with it last night."

"Can we just dance, please?"

Before he could respond the music changed and Amy was there, pulling Jessa from his arms. "Let her go, Garrett. Go back to the table with the guys. Us girls are gonna get our groove on!" Amy laughed as she tugged on Jessa's hand.

Garrett watched as the women went to the center of the floor and started swaying with the music, oblivious of the couples dancing around them. He couldn't help but smile at the delight on Jessa's face. She seemed to be enjoying herself and he'd been a total ass. Resigned to the fact that he wouldn't be dancing with her anytime soon, he went back to the table.

"What the fuck are you doing?" Tyler eyed him as he slid a tumbler of whiskey into Garrett's waiting hand.

"I could ask you the same question." Garrett's eyes were glued on Jessa. She moved her body like she'd been made to dance. He didn't think it possible to get harder than he already was, but that's what she did to him. Two fucking days he'd known her and she'd turned him into a walking hard-on. She raised her arms over her head and rolled her body from her shoulders to her hips. Fuuuuuuck.

"Are you listening to me?" Tyler punched him hard in the arm.

"Ow! What the hell?"

"Pay attention. Stop drooling over Jessa. And don't worry. Jim and Miles are too busy ogling their wives to notice the eye fuck you've got going on. Seriously man. Tone that shit down."

Garrett didn't take kindly to being told what to do, not by Tyler. Especially when it came to Jessa. "How about you mind your own fucking business."

"Or what?" Tyler sneered. "You gonna kick my ass? We aren't in fucking college. You need to get control of yourself. And I mean now."

"Leave it alone, Ty."

Tyler shook his head, his mouth drawn into a thin line. "You stupid motherfucker. We've been friends a long time. I'm gonna give you a break since your dick seems to be overriding your brain tonight. You need to get your shit straight, Garrett. You're playing with fire with that one. Christ man, this isn't how you want to start your professional career. She isn't some chick you can play around with and then walk away from. You hear me? If you need to get laid, there are plenty of women in town that would jump at the chance. Find one, get your rocks off, and forget about Jessa Montgomery."

Garrett gripped his glass so hard he feared it'd break. It was either that or he was going to punch Tyler in the face. Repeatedly. "When did you get so damned self-righteous? You wouldn't know what to do with the same woman twice. Now you think to lecture me about my sex life?" Garrett downed the rest of his whiskey, ignoring Tyler's threatening growl. "Save your speeches. I'm done listening." Garrett pushed back his chair.

In fact, he was done with this whole fucking night.

CHAPTER SIX

The lobby was packed with people. Jessa only recognized a few as being from the ball club. She'd be surprised if the majority of the men weren't locals, here to get in on the action. There had to be at least three women to every man. Add a little music and the hotel could charge a cover to get into the lobby. Good lord. There was more skin showing than in all the strip clubs in Vegas.

Jessa dared a glance at Garrett, wondering if he'd react. It was more than obvious that most of these women were here for one purpose. To land — or lay — a baseball player. And she'd thought *men* were bad. Jeez.

It didn't take long for the horde to notice them. Conversations halted and heated glances were tossed their way as Garrett lead them into the hotel. Jessa's cheeks grew warm as she realized men were watching her as much as women were leering at Garrett. Her heart fluttered when he entwined their fingers, his expression fierce, possessive, and he tugged her closer to his side. She flexed her hand, his hold cutting off the blood supply to her fingers. He growled a warning, but at least he eased his grip.

He was making her crazy.

He'd dragged her from the dance floor, insisting he had an early day tomorrow, saying it was his job to get her back safely. She hadn't missed his not-so-subtle dig about their relationship being about a job. He'd waited, not so patiently, while she said her goodbyes to everyone before he hauled her out of there, only to remain silent the entire way back to the hotel.

The tension between them was palpable. She couldn't read him. Had no idea what had his jaw clenched and his shoulders tight. But if he kept dragging her around like an errant child, she was going to scream.

They passed the front desk and a woman stepped in front of him, impeding their progress. Tall and slender, the woman tossed her long auburn hair over her shoulder, revealing the top curve of her breast. The woman leaned in, boldly sliding her hand down Garrett's chest. "Aren't you Garrett Donovan?" she asked, her fingers gliding down to toy with the buckle on his belt.

Jessa fumed at the blatant display, irrational jealousy biting at her heart. The woman ignored her, choosing instead to wrap herself around Garrett's other arm and making the most ridiculous giggle sound Jessa had ever heard. "You're so much bigger up close." The brazen hussy actually licked her lips, not even trying to hide the fact that she was peeking around to stare at Garrett's crotch.

Jessa rolled her eyes. For chrissake, did the woman have no shame?

To make matters worse, Garrett transformed, the angry lines of his face gliding into a charming smile. "I'll take that as a compliment, darlin'. Thank you."

Ever the fucking gentleman.

"You want company tonight?" The woman's voice was low, seductive. She squeezed his arm between her breasts. "I'll put a smile on that handsome face of yours."

He passed a hot, angry glance at Jessa. "Oh, I definitely want company tonight," he murmured.

Jessa sucked in a breath. She had no claim on him, but that didn't stop her heart from seizing at the thought of him in this woman's arms. Well, if Garrett wanted to stand here and flirt, that was his choice, but she damn sure didn't have to stay here and watch. Her stomach jumped, her dinner threatening to make a reappearance.

"I can get back on my own." Her voice shook, her nerves on edge. She didn't want him to stay here, but she really didn't get a say in that, now did she? Goddamn it, she wouldn't cry.

Would. Not.

He didn't belong to her, couldn't belong to her. She yanked her hand from his. "Have fun."

Garrett snagged her wrist in a painful grip. Jessa cried out in protest, turning as he eased out of the other woman's grip. "Thank you for the kind offer, ma'am." His gaze never strayed from Jessa. "But, as you can see, my hands are full."

The woman's eyes narrowed on Jessa as if sizing up the competition. "If you change your mind, I'm Cindy." She purred. "I'll be around." With one last glare to Jessa, the woman sauntered away, no doubt in search of her next victim.

Garrett jerked Jessa back to his side. His jaw was rigid as if he were grinding his teeth. Something he did a lot around her, she'd noticed. His hand pressed against the skin of her lower back, and his warmth startled her. Made her want to arch like a cat, begging him to stroke her. He kept the pressure firm as he directed her toward the bank of elevators. He was so confident, so sure she'd follow. And she would. She couldn't seem to resist him, but that didn't mean she had to make it easy.

"Garrett, let go. You're hurting me." He wasn't, but she twisted her arm until he was forced to release her anyway. "What is your problem?"

"Not here." He ushered her along, weaving around the crowd until they stood in front of the elevators.

The elevator doors opened and Garrett steered her inside. He maneuvered them to the corner, placing her back against his front. People continued to fill the space and Jessa found herself pressed against his warm, hard body. She shifted her feet, trying to make more room for him, to escape the sensation of his body against hers.

"Be still!" he hissed in her ear. He jerked her back, his fingers digging into her hips until she knew she'd bare his mark.

Her heart hammered, her chest constricting, making it difficult to breathe in the crowded space. His impressive erection seared her lower back. He released her hips, his hands slipping through the opening of her dress and settling on her waist. Her breath caught as his fingers traced feather light circles on her abdomen.

Her body ignited. Flames licked at her skin, her breasts growing heavy and uncomfortable in the confines of her dress. Desire exploded, bolts of electricity racing through her veins. Nerve endings came alive, jumping to the surface and preening beneath his wicked fingers.

She fidgeted, twisting her hands around the strap of her bag until it cut off her circulation. She wanted to get to her room, crawl into bed, and forget this night ever happened. In the morning, she'd call her dad and tell him she was coming home. He'd have to rely on someone else. If she stayed, she'd lose more than a night on the dance floor. The powerful man standing behind her would steal her heart. She would ruin them both.

His fingers danced across her skin, stealing her breath, stealing her will to resist. Garrett mastered her. Standing in an elevator full of people, his touch had reduced her to a puddle of need. For him. Anything he wanted, however he wanted. Consequences be damned.

Her pussy throbbed, flooded with arousal as she fought to remain still. He teased along the edge of her garter belt and her stomach rolled, clenched under his touch.

Oh God, there was no way he hadn't felt that. He knew. He had to know what he was doing to her.

Garrett didn't seem to care that they weren't alone. Moving upward, his finger tickled the underside of her breast. Jesus, of all nights to forgo undergarments. She held her breath, wondering if he dared to touch her sensitive nipples. She was dying for him to touch her. The effort it took to breathe normally was exhausting. Jessa glared at the glowing numbers, willing the elevator to go faster. Arousal bordered on pain as she counted the floors and tried desperately to hold on to her dignity.

The elevator doors opened and Garrett jerked his hands away. He pressed against her back again, urging her forward. "Move out, Jessa."

The command in his voice took her by surprise. Aggression and anger poured from his expression, giving her pause. She had no idea what his problem was. More importantly, she didn't know if she should be worried or not.

Garrett took her hand and all but dragged her behind him. She tried to dig her heels in. "Garrett, wait. Where are we going? My room isn't on this floor."

He rounded on her. "No, *my* room is on this floor. Now, you can either walk or I'll throw you over my shoulder. Either way, you're coming with me."

"Garrett, I —"

He growled, bent and pushed his shoulder into her stomach, scooping her up.

"Garrett!" Jessa raised her head enough to see if anyone had followed them into the hallway, relieved to find it empty.

"I warned you."

Jessa braced her hands against his lower back, shifting her hips to lessen the bite of his shoulder.

"Hold still." His palm came down on her backside.

"Hey! Who do you think you are? You know, you're being really fucking annoying tonight. Put me down." She slapped his ass hard while struggling to keep her breasts from falling out of her dress. As much as his Neanderthal tactics pissed her off, she was shaken from his touch in the elevator. Turned on.

He stopped. His hand skimmed the back of her thigh, up over her hip. She bit back a moan as he knelt to put her back on her feet. She straightened her dress and tried to get a hold of herself.

With a look of warning, he made quick work of the keycard and all but shoved her inside.

She hadn't even gotten all the way into the room before he went off. "What the hell did you think you were doing?"

"Could you be more specific?" Arrogant jerk, thinking he could toss her around like a sack of potatoes. Who did he think he was?

He paced the floor in front of her. "Tonight. Dancing. Flirting with Tyler. That ... that dress." He waved a hand over her. "And I use the term loosely, of course. I'm not sure that scrap of material you're wearing qualifies as an actual dress."

"Where do you get off judging anything I do? I happen to like this dress." She smoothed her hands down her body, his eyes tracking every move.

He snorted. "You and every man in the vicinity of you."

"Need I remind you that going to dinner was *your* idea? And as for the dancing ..." She shrugged a shoulder. "When in Rome."

"And Tyler?" He ground out.

"He's cute, and a good dancer. Why wouldn't I have fun with him? I'm single. Free to dance with whoever the hell I want. Jesus! You were the one who said I didn't know how to have fun, then the minute I do ... what is your issue, Garrett?"

"You let him touch you." His voice was harsh, fierce.

"Is that what this is about? Because you think —" She threw her hands up, glaring at him. "We were *dancing* Garrett. Kind of hard to do without touching."

He took a step toward her. "I don't *think* anything. His hands were all over you tonight, touching the skin that I ... damn it. Tell me, Jess. Do you prefer Tyler's touch to mine?"

Jessa stared at him, his eyes filled with a mixture of anger and lust. A look that told her if she wanted, she could be in his bed tonight. And oh, she wanted.

For once in her life, she would take what she wanted. No holding back, no allowing fear of judgment to get in her way. She was going for it.

"Tyler's touch." She kept her voice low, seductive. "His hands on me." She ran her hands over her breasts, down her stomach, her movement slow, methodical. "His body against mine as we danced." She rolled her hips as she smoothed the dress over her curves. She closed her eyes for a second, as if reliving the moment, before dropping her hands to her sides and giving him a dry stare.

"I didn't feel anything special. Tyler doesn't do it for me, Garrett. I could simply relax and enjoy myself. But you," she jabbed his chest. "You turn me inside out. One look and I'm ready for you. My nipples get hard thinking about you, so when you put your hands on me tonight, yeah. It was too much. All I could think about was your kiss, what it would feel like to have your hands all over my skin. How you would taste if I took you into my mouth. One touch, Garrett, and I needed you so badly that I didn't think I could take another minute."

"You make me insane, you know that?" He stepped closer, his hands gripping her arms and lifting her against him. "I'm going to kiss you, Jessa. Tell me no." He closed his eyes, resting his forehead against hers. "Goddamn it, tell me no."

Yeah, no way that was happening. She hadn't stopped thinking about the last time they'd kissed. She wanted more, and she wasn't going to wait another minute. She tipped her head and pressed her mouth to his.

* * *

Garrett was losing his fucking mind. The feel of her soft mouth on his sent a bolt of lightning straight to his dick. He'd been hard since the moment she'd opened the door tonight, that damn dress taunting him with her every movement. Making him crazy to know if she wore anything underneath.

"Damn it, Jessa." He ripped his lips from hers. "I can't. You're ... fuck. We can't do this." He needed to get away from her. He needed to get inside her.

Either way, he was fucked.

Jessa stood there, her expression stunned. Her chest rose and fell in rapid succession to his. "Are you serious?"

"You should go." His voice was hard, determined, a last ditch effort to do the right thing before he destroyed everything. It took every bit of his restraint not to throw her over the arm of the couch and sink into her from behind. And he wouldn't stop there. Not even close. The way he felt right now, he'd take her every way imaginable and a few ways he might make up as they go along. If she didn't go now.

"I don't want to go. It's just you and me here, Garrett. Just you and me." Her eyes filled with tears. "Don't deny us this night. Please, Garrett."

Need filled her teary eyes. Her mumbled words were his downfall. There'd be no more tears tonight. Only pleasure. He'd make her forget all about her tears because now, there'd be no walking away.

He yanked her to his chest, lifting her feet from the floor as he ground his hips against her. Even fully clothed, the heat from her pussy burned him, set his blood on fire. He took her mouth, forcing his way in until her taste flowed over his tongue.

She went limp in his arms, his body molding to her every curve. He couldn't wait. Mindless of anything except getting inside her, Garrett reached between them and loosened his belt.

Her hands, soft and tentative, threaded around his neck. A shudder racked his body as she toyed with the ends of his hair. She scraped her nails along his neck. The little vixen dug into his shoulders, her tongue more insistent in his mouth.

He cupped the back of her neck, holding her in place while he dined on the most delicious mouth he'd ever tasted.

"You taste so sweet, so warm and inviting. I could spend all night kissing you, Jess." He teased his tongue across her mouth. "Your lips are so full and pretty. Red and swollen from my kisses. Do you have any idea what that does to me? Damn, I can't wait to see those lips wrapped around my cock." He looked into her eyes, glazed over with desire. "You're so beautiful, Jessa. Can I see the rest of you? Will you show me what I want to see, baby?"

"God, Garrett." She was breathless, straining in his arms.

"Relax, baby," he murmured against her lips. "I've got you. We're going to take the edge off, and then we'll play." He reached behind her neck, releasing the catch of her dress. He stepped back, his heart hammering in his chest as the material fluttered down her body and landed in a shimmering pool at her feet.

Sweet Mary, Mother of God.

Jessa stood before him, black thigh-highs secured by garters that hung from a tiny scrap of black lace around her hips. The rest of her glorious body was bare to his gaze, exactly as he'd imagined. Her breasts were beautiful, a perfect fit for his hands. Darkened nipples tipped the tanned mounds. All he could think about was drawing each one in his mouth until she writhed beneath him. The bare lips of her pussy glistened, beckoning him to touch her, taste her. He cleared his throat. "Where are your panties?"

Her lips quirked. "Didn't wear any."

He groaned. She was going to kill him. "It's a damn good thing I didn't know that earlier, or we'd have never made it out of the restaurant. Hell, we may have never made it *to* the restaurant. Jesus, it was hard enough knowing you weren't wearing a bra. Come here, Jessa, I need to touch you." He spun her in a slow circle, taking in every inch of her. He ran his palm over the satiny skin of her ass. "Did you wear this get up for me, princess?"

"Maybe."

He pulled her to him, holding her arms behind her back. Her breath hitched, her eyes darkened. She liked it rough. He saw it in her gaze, in the way she clawed at him. And God help him, he'd give it to her. "You did, didn't you?" He bent his head and flicked the tip of his tongue over her nipple. "Mmm. So sweet. Tell me you want me. God, Jessa," he said and sucked the tight bud deep into his mouth and felt the last of his restraint go.

CHAPTER SEVEN

"I want you." Three little words, the best she could do when she was about to combust into a pile of ash on his carpet. Her body trembled, her knees threatening to buckle. If he hadn't slipped an arm around her waist she'd be a puddle on the floor.

Garrett feasted on her breasts. He cupped them, brushed his thumbs across the sensitive peaks before rolling each bud between his fingers and she was lost. In this moment, it wasn't wrong for them to be together. She wasn't bad for him. Her passion not a detriment to his career, his life.

Nothing existed except his touch.

She reached for his shoulders, her nails digging through his shirt, needing more. She cried out as he pinched her nipples and sparks shot through her breasts, the sensation echoing in her clit.

He pushed his leg between hers and pressed up, raising her until she was riding his thigh. The pressure and friction against her naked flesh was too much. Her face heated, knowing the moisture weeping from her pussy would drench his slacks.

His chest rumbled. "As beautiful as your skin is, all rosy and pink, I won't have any shame from you." He arched his hips, the hot, rigid length of his erection pressing against her hip. "You feel how hard I am? You did that to me, Jessa." He nibbled along her jaw line. "Don't be embarrassed with me, baby. Never with me."

His mouth slanted over hers, his lips moist and warm. She opened at his urging and his tongue took over — licking, tasting, taking everything she had and demanding more. More was good. More was imperative. Like breathing.

He shifted until his fingers teased up the inside of her thigh. "Open your legs, Jess. Let me see how wet you are for me."

She choked on a breath as he found her sensitive flesh. His gentle fingers caressed her slit, spreading her arousal over her folds. A whimper tore from her throat as he touched her clit, fire igniting in her womb as he flicked the engorged bud.

"Jesus, I love that you're bare here. That there won't be anything between me and your sweet, sweet pussy." He circled her opening before easing a finger deep inside.

She raised on her toes, his wicked finger teasing her before retreating again. She was burning, her vagina contracting around him. She was close. So close. Perspiration broke out on her skin as she clung to him.

"You are so beautiful. Have I ever told you that? And your taste." Garrett leaned back, putting the finger covered in her juices into his mouth. "The sweetest honey." His eyes drifted closed as if he was eating ambrosia. With a hungry growl, Garrett scooped her into his arms. "I need you now, Jess."

A surge of pleasure buzzed through her. It had embarrassed her at first, but the reality of it was she loved his dirty talk, loved that he shared his desire with her. Loved that he was as crazy with need as she was.

She wrapped her arms around him and snuggled into his neck, letting his scent fill her nose. She could get drunk on him. She delighted at his shiver as she ran her tongue over the cords of his neck, snickering as he stumbled through the door. He released her legs and she slid down his body, relishing the contrast of his large body against her much smaller one. Growing up with only her father had turned Jessa into somewhat of a tomboy. She was strong, solid. But right now, she'd never felt more like a woman. Garrett made her feel ... soft. Feminine. Desirable.

"You think that's funny?"

"I like that I can affect you, because you're sure playing havoc with me."

"Is that right?" His laugh was dark, sensual.

He'd said no shame. He was offering her a chance to be bold, free herself to experience the pleasure promised in his gaze. Pleasure she wanted to return.

She opened the button of his slacks, slowly drawing the zipper down. "It's my turn to taste you." She kicked off her shoes and went to her knees in front of him. She smiled at his curse as she drew his pants down. His heavy erection sprung free, mere inches from her lips. She sucked in a breath. He was large. Larger than any man she'd been with before. Her pussy throbbed in anticipation, even as nerves attacked her stomach.

His head rolled back on his shoulders as she wrapped her hand around him, learning the feel of his rigid length. Hot, silken, flesh-covered steel as she stroked him from base to tip. A drop of moisture appeared and she couldn't resist reaching out for it. Using the tip of her tongue, she brushed over his slit, moaning as she got her first taste of him. His tangy essence rolled over her and she wanted more. She wanted it all.

"Shit, Jess. Suck it, baby. Take me in that hot little mouth." He nudged his swollen cock against her.

She opened, wrapping her lips around the broad crest. His thighs bunched as he tried to press forward, but she wasn't having it. He wasn't denying her this chance to savor him.

"Ah, Christ." Garrett's breath was ragged. "That's it, Jess. Take me deeper, baby."

He filled her, her lips stretching tight around his thick length. She arched her neck, sucking him in as far as she could. Her hand stroking in tandem as she moved.

Garrett's hands tangled in her hair. "Just like that, Jess. That's so good."

His praise drove her need higher. Cream flowed from her body as she swiped her tongue over the bloated head before shoving him deep again. He nudged the back of her throat and she fought not to gag. Her eyes watered and she drew air through her nose, refusing to release him.

She swallowed.

"Fuck!" Garrett yelled out above her. He pulled on her hair, sending a delicious tingle through her scalp as he jerked himself from her.

Without warning, he picked her up and tossed her back on the bed. She couldn't speak. Couldn't think. She arched her hips, a silent plea.

He caressed up her leg, releasing first one garter, then the next, rolling her thigh highs down and pulling them off. He reached for the garter belt; she raised her hips and he swept it from her.

He stared down at her, his gaze predatory, hungry. He growled, pressing his hands along the inside of her legs, opening her. Then, his mouth was on her. Fast, hard, like a man possessed.

She cried out, twitched, her body bursting into flames, as his tongue dove deep into her opening. "Garrett!" Pure, unadulterated need bled from her voice. His hands pushed at the back of her legs, holding her in place as she struggled to get closer.

"You taste like heaven, baby." She twisted the covers in her fists, as he pushed a finger into her. "And so hot." He added another finger and then another as he started a slow, smooth rhythm that stole her breath. "Perfect."

His mouth was perfect.

He sucked her clit into his mouth. Her legs shook, the tension building in her body too much to bear. She was so close. "Garrett, please," she whimpered.

He raised his head, his chin glistening with her juices. "Tell me what you want, baby."

"I need to come. Please, Garrett." She didn't care that she was begging. She didn't care that she'd never asked a man to make her come, *begged* a man to make her come.

She couldn't care about anything except the riot that was happening in her body. The fire Garrett had stoked, her nerve endings vibrating as if trying to escape. She was turned inside out and willing to give him whatever he wanted.

Sweat ran from her temples as he curled his fingers, stimulating that sweet, sensitive area deep within her. She gasped as he moved a finger from her pussy, trailing it back to press against the tiny hidden entrance of her ass. He held fast as she tried to squirm away. "What are you —?"

She screamed as his finger twirled around the puckered skin and she broke into a million pieces. Her muscles drew tight, pulling her back off the bed as her orgasm exploded through her. Stars appeared behind her eyes, pleasure overwhelming in its intensity.

Garrett came over her then, his clothes gone.

"You're gorgeous when you come, baby." He was panting as he positioned himself at her entrance. "Show me again." He braced himself above her and arched his hips, pressing the head of his cock into her.

Her body opened for him, her flesh sensitized from her release. He stretched her; tiny sparks of pain mixed with pleasure as he started a slow rhythm.

"God, Jessa. Fuck. So tight." He moved in shallow strokes, working his length inside her. His face was drawn, his jaw clenched tight.

She wrapped her legs around his hips, her desire for him growing with every silken stroke. He was driving her mad, taking his time, working into her inch by slow inch.

"More. Need more." She was reduced to single syllables, her desire fogging her ability to think of anything beyond her blinding need.

"You gonna come for me again, baby?" Garrett forced his hips forward with a grunt, burying himself to the hilt.

"Yes!" She cried out as molten steel pierced her tender tissue. Her vagina gripped him, pulsated and wept as her release washed over her, leaving her breathless.

Her contractions held him tight, his groan filling the room. "God, Jessa. I need to move, baby. You okay?"

The fact that he was concerned about her warmed her heart. She laced her hands behind his neck and brought his mouth to hers. "Fuck me, Garrett. Fuck me hard," she whispered against his lips.

His eyes flared a second before he crushed his mouth to hers. She opened, drawing his tongue, his essence into her, until her throat burned with the need to breathe.

An animalistic sound rumbled as he pulled away, his chest heaving and wet as she ran her hands over him. The air was heavy with sweat and sex as his hips pistoned against hers. His pelvis rubbed her clit with each stroke. "Come with me, baby," he ground out.

"Can't. Not again." She shook her head in denial.

He pushed back to his knees, draping her legs over his hips, and continued to pound into her. "You can. Come with me," he demanded and pressed his thumb to her clit.

Jessa flew. Not the intense tidal wave of before, but a gentle crest that melted her, scattered her particles on the wind. She soared, her body light, nonexistent. From a hundred miles away she heard Garrett's shout as he gained his own release.

She closed her eyes and breathed deep, reveling in the feel of him over her. She could get used to this.

Garrett moved from her, rolling to his side. Jessa turned with him, content to curl up in his arms. He held her as she gained her breath, as her world turned right-side up again.

Feeling vulnerable in the aftermath, she arched her neck, searching for his gaze. His wide-eyed stare met hers and Jessa's heart sank.

The panic was undeniable. Oh, she knew that look.

It was the look of a man who realized he'd just made a mistake.

* * *

Garrett felt raw, exposed.

Drained.

He couldn't form a coherent sentence right now if his life depended on it. Fuck, he'd never come so hard in his life. He may have even blacked out for a second or two.

Her moans and tiny whimpers of pleasure, her hungry pleas, drove him wild. She'd tied him in knots, twisted his guts until he couldn't breathe but for her. Until she'd been all that mattered.

Something happened as he'd buried himself inside her. Something he didn't have a name for. Something he didn't want to think about.

It scared the shit out of him.

He cradled Jessa, held her close to his chest as he recovered from the power of his release. She stretched her neck and he met her sleepy gaze. He was in awe of her. She was gorgeous like this. Her tousled hair fell over her shoulder. Her neck and throat showed the signs of his stubble. Her kiss-swollen lips were too much of a temptation.

He leaned in, but she turned away. Not what he'd expected after the mind-blowing sex they'd shared.

"Jess, you okay, baby?"

The smile she offered didn't reassure him.

"That was fun, thanks."

Fun?

"Jessa —"

"I need to go." She sat up and threw her legs over the side of the bed.

Garrett caught her around the waist and brought her back against his chest. "Don't."

Jessa laughed and wiggled out of his arms. She moved from the bed, her skin still slick from their passion.

"Stay. Shower with me."

"I have to get back to my room." She looked pointedly at his latex covered cock. An expression resembling relief swept over her features before she replaced it with a grin. "You really had me out of it, because I have no idea when you had time to do that. I'm glad you did, thank you. At least one of us kept their head."

"That's debatable," he mumbled, wary of her tone. "You aren't protected?" If she knew how close he'd been to forgetting, she wouldn't look so grateful.

"I'm on the pill, but … you know."

Garrett rolled off the bed, removed the condom and tossed it into the wastebasket. "If that's another dig about my supposed whorish ways, you can save it. It's not my style." She skirted around him as he reached for her again. "In fact, you're the first woman I've had sex with in a long time."

She arched a brow. "Not many men would admit to something like that. How long?" she asked, collecting her hose, garters and shoes.

He didn't want to have this conversation right now. He wanted to pull her back to bed and feel her warmth against him. He wanted to sink back into her heat and lose himself in her. "I've got nothing to be ashamed about. I've been busy, and quick one-nighters don't do it for me anymore." Meaning he'd have more than one night with her. "And it's been over a year."

"A year, really?" There was a subtle tremor in her voice. "That's a long time."

He pulled on a pair of shorts and followed her to the living room. She shimmied into her dress and he watched as she reached up to fasten the hook behind her head. Her nipples hardened under his gaze, poking through the delicate fabric. "What about you?"

She laughed. "Longer than that."

"So, we're both safe then." He watched her with a wary eye. He didn't know what was in her mind, but he figured he wasn't going to like it.

She took a deep breath and faced him. "It doesn't matter. We can't do this again."

Anger tore through him at her words. "Bullshit."

She gave him an irritated look. "Be reasonable about this. We shared an incredible experience, but that's all. You have to focus on your game. Spring training, remember? We have jobs to do, and we can't afford to be distracted. Plus, my dad would freak if he found out. You don't need that kind of hassle."

"You've got to be fucking kidding me. You can't throw that shit at me now."

Her back stiffened. "Please, I'm not telling you anything you don't already know."

Garrett gripped the back of his neck, confused as hell. "I'm not sure what's going on, but you don't have to go. We can figure this out, Jessa ... stay."

Sadness flickered in her expression before her features went blank. "I can't. You know I can't. We had an itch, and we scratched it. Let's not make a big deal about it." She pressed a quick kiss to his lips before she hurried toward the door. "Good night, Garrett."

He watched as the door closed behind her.

An itch? A fucking itch?

Frozen in place, he replayed the last few minutes. She'd been right there with him the whole time. The pleasure between them a living, breathing entity in the room. And now she was running off? Minutes after they'd both come?

What the hell?

Maybe she was right. They both knew the limitations, yet they'd broken the rules because the pull between them was too strong.

He wandered through his suite, avoiding the bedroom. If he had to see the rumpled sheets, smell the sweet scent of their arousal, he'd end up going after her. Dragging her back and fucking her until she was too tired to walk away from him again.

Shit. She was in him now. Her taste in his mouth, her scent on his skin. He was nowhere near done with her.

Not even close.

CHAPTER EIGHT

"Fuck!" Garrett slammed the end of his bat into the dirt after another ball whizzed by. Anger fueled his system. Anger that had nothing to do with his worthless attempt at batting practice and everything to do with a certain woman who was driving him out of his mind.

He removed his helmet, resisting the urge to hurl it toward the dugout. It was one thing for Jessa to up and leave him last night, but now she was avoiding him, and he'd be damned if he could figure out why.

The message she'd left him this morning said she wouldn't be riding to the park with him and would meet up with him later. It wasn't that he had a problem finding his own way. It was about time he rented a car anyway. It would give the guys one less thing to give him shit about. The problem was, he hadn't realized how much he'd been looking forward to seeing her until she'd ditched him. Strike one.

He went to the locker room and fell into the chair next to his locker. He unfastened his shin guard and shoved it into his bag.

Jessa had been a no-show all afternoon. He knew she was in the park. He could feel her eyes on him in a way that rattled him as much as it pissed him off. She'd not made any effort to seek him out. No 'hello'. No 'how's your day?' Nothing. Strike two.

"You've got to get that girl out of your head, buddy."

Garrett straightened as Tyler pulled a chair close and straddled it between his legs. "Don't you have anything better to do than harass me about something that's none of your business?"

Tyler shrugged. "There are rules here. Unwritten, sure, but that doesn't make them any less critical to your career."

"Since when do you give a shit about anything except how many women you can fuck at one time?"

Tyler laughed. "Good point. But who I fuck isn't up for discussion right now."

"My sex life isn't either." Garrett stripped off his shirt and tossed it into his bag. He pulled out a bottle of water and drank it down, wishing it were something stronger. Much stronger. Maybe then he could ignore the fact that Tyler was right. Garrett should have stayed away from Jessa. He should have played it straight and stayed focused. Too late for all that now.

"Did you fuck her?"

Garrett glanced around to make sure they hadn't been overheard, and found himself counting to ten. In the past that kind of question wouldn't have affected him. They were guys. It was a typical guy question to ask. So why did he have the sudden urge to knock all of Tyler's teeth out?

"Don't push me on this, Tyler." Garrett was running low on patience. He needed a shower and a cold beer, and he was damn tired of arguing with his friend.

"Right, because you've got it all under control. Tell me something, Garrett. What happens when TJ finds out you fucked his only daughter? What do you think he'll do when you break that girl's heart?"

"Who said I'm gonna break her heart?" And why the hell was he still talking about this?

Tyler gave him a skeptical look. "So ... what? You think you'll have some fun? Fuck a few times and that's it?" His expression turned thoughtful. "Hmm, I never pegged Jessa as a blow and go kind of girl."

"That's enough," Garrett snapped. "You ever talk about Jessa like that again and I'll make sure you regret it. I'll admit, I don't have any idea what I'm doing, but I do know what happens between me and Jessa is just that — between me and Jessa. If you value our friendship, Ty, back the hell off."

Something akin to understanding flashed in Tyler's eyes before he stood and clapped a hand on Garrett's shoulder. "It's *because* I value our friendship that I'm in your face about this. Your family is counting on you. Your team is counting on you. Do the right thing."

Tyler walked away and Garrett dropped his head into his hands.

Do the right thing. He wasn't sure he knew what the right thing was anymore. Jessa had swooped in and turned him inside out in a matter of days. Right or wrong, they weren't finished. Not by a long shot. He'd tasted heaven last night and, if he had his way, he'd be dining again tonight.

A chime sounded and he reached for his cell. His blood pressure went up a notch as he read the text message from Jessa.

> *Tough batting practice.*
> *Looks like you need some rest.*
> *I'll see you tomorrow.*

Fuck. That.

Strike three, baby.

She wasn't going to run from him. Not after last night. He knew the impossible situation they were in and right now, he didn't give a shit. He was pissed off, hard as a fucking brick, and distracted as hell.

A smile tugged at his lips as he thought of his next move.

> *You'll see me sooner than that.*

He pressed send, knowing he'd have to hurry before she hightailed it out of there. He finished changing as fast as he could, wishing for a shower, but he didn't want to risk missing her.

There was only one place she could be. Her dad's skybox gave her the greatest advantage. She could watch his practice and avoid him at the same time.

By the time Garrett got there, his patience had reached its limits. His gaze zeroed in on her the minute he walked through the door. Facing the windows overlooking the field, she was dressed in a T-shirt that hugged her curves, barely meeting the top of her low-rise shorts. Her hair was pulled back, no doubt in an effort to keep cool in this unusual spring heat.

There were two men with her, men he recognized but couldn't place. But it didn't matter who they were as long as they were gone.

As if she'd sensed him, Jessa straightened, affording him a glimpse of the mouthwatering skin of her back. God, he loved her back. The feminine curve of her spine softened under the sleek muscles that went taut as she turned around. He gritted his teeth as the men next to her noticed the movement as well. Garrett hoped he wouldn't have to kick their asses, but if they didn't raise their eyes back to a respectable level, it was a serious possibility.

Garrett maneuvered around tables set with food, sparing a glance toward the sitting area and finding it empty. Great. Once he got rid of Frick and Frack, they'd be alone.

"I need the room," Garrett demanded without so much as a greeting.

Jessa flushed. "What's the matter with you? Can't you see I'm busy?"

"We can do this now, or I can drag your ass out of here and we can do this somewhere else," he challenged, crossing his arms over his chest.

"Yes, well," she sliced her hand through the air. "After your performance out there today, I'd agree there are some things we need to talk about." Her gaze darted between him and the men who were watching with great interest.

Her attempt to cover him was laughable. Anyone who was paying attention could feel the tension. A sexual energy so strong he had to fist his hands at his sides to avoid pulling her against him.

"My performance." He dragged out the word, rubbing his chin, pretending to consider her words. He let his gaze drop to her breasts and damn if his dick didn't about jump out of his shorts. "I think a replay is in order."

She huffed a breath. "Gentlemen, if you would excuse us for a minute, please?"

Self-preservation a thing of the past, Garrett responded, "Oh, we're gonna need more than a minute, sweetheart."

Jesus, he'd never been possessive a day in his life, yet here he was … marking his territory.

His.

Jessa glared at him, annoyance plastered all over her face as Frick and Frack said quick goodbyes and shuffled out.

"What the hell do you think you're doing? You may not care about what other people think, but I have to. For both our sakes." Anger sparked in her eyes as she jabbed a finger at him. "You better hope those guys don't talk about your little stunt, or we'll have a shit load of explaining to do."

"Is that why you've been avoiding me?"

She crossed her arms. "I have no idea what you mean."

"Because you care about what other people think?"

"I haven't been —"

"Cut the shit, Jess. You've been avoiding me and you know it. I want to know why." And they weren't leaving this room until he had an answer.

"Oh, I don't know, Garrett. Maybe it's because I didn't want to see more of your disappointment." She grimaced. "The look that reminds me you made a mistake by having sex with me. The same look you had on your face *last night*."

The hurt in her eyes settled hard in the pit of his stomach.

"Disappointment? What the hell are you talking about? Is that why you ran out?" He blew out a breath when she didn't answer.

His voice turned harsh with frustration. "Christ, Jessa. I'm not into playing games. You shouldn't have taken off like that." The thought that she'd believed he'd been sorry ripped a hole in his chest. Nothing could've been further from the truth.

"It was a mistake. You know it. I know it. It doesn't matter anymore. Let's move on."

"The fuck it doesn't matter! Is that really what you think?" He couldn't keep the incredulity from his voice. "Look me in the eye and tell me last night didn't mean anything, Jessa."

She raised her chin. "You know what? Fuck you."

"Oh, sweetheart. We'll get to that, don't you worry. But first, we need to get a few things straight."

Her hand fluttered across her throat. "What do you want from me?"

Garrett held tight to the temper threatening to erupt. "I want you to fucking talk to me! If there's something bothering you, or something I've done to hurt you then you need to fucking tell me about it. Not leave me wondering what the hell is going on. And avoiding me just pisses me off."

He stormed back to the door and flipped the lock, taking a moment to breathe. He schooled his expression as he turned back to her. "You think I'm sorry about last night? I don't know what you saw, sweetheart, but I promise you, it wasn't regret."

Every muscle in his body screamed in protest as he held himself in check. "Mind-blowing, intense pleasure ..." He walked a slow, wide circle around her, herding her away from the windows. "An orgasm so powerful, I swear my balls are still recovering." He gave her a look to assure her that he'd recovered enough. "These are things I felt last night, sweetheart. Not regret."

His dick throbbed, fully engorged in his shorts. "I can still feel you, Jessa." He kept his voice soft, soothing, as if he were coaxing a scared rabbit. "The warmth of your skin, the taste of you on my tongue." Ignoring her sharp intake of breath, he backed her into the wall.

Not touching her was no longer an option. "Does that feel like regret, baby?" He rubbed his erection against her stomach, groaning as pleasure spiked through his balls. He wanted nothing more than to lay her out and shove his dick so far into her that she'd wear his imprint for hours, days. He wanted to touch and taste every inch of her.

He wanted things he knew were impossible.

For now, he'd settle for making her come until she couldn't see straight.

"Last night threw me, Jess." He trailed his lips across her jaw. "You took my breath away, and I won't apologize for being a little dazed afterward any more than I'll apologize for this." He pushed her shirt up, groaning as he exposed the sexiest red lace bra he'd ever seen. He tugged the edges down, and sucked a nipple into his mouth.

Sweet heaven.

Every cell in his body screamed to take her, but he couldn't. Not yet. He wanted her hot and desperate, with him every step of the way.

Her soft moan was music to his ears. He went from one nipple to the other, lingering, tasting, teasing the tormented buds until they were peaked and rosy.

"I love your nipples, Jess. So pretty." He rolled one between his fingers. "Pink and glistening from my mouth. Like your pussy is going to be."

"Garrett." She dug her nails into his shoulders and his dick thickened even more.

"I'm not going to fuck you, princess. Not here. Not now."

She whimpered in protest and he pulled at the button on her shorts.

"I should walk away and leave you as fucking needy as I've been all day. Make you wait. Make you crazy." His heart pounded in his throat as the sound of her zipper filled the space between them. Even as he said the words, he knew he'd never be able to do it. He was dying to feel her, if not around his dick then clenching his fingers.

"Why are you doing this to me?" She arched into his hand.

"What am I doing, baby? Am I making you wet?" His breath was coming in short spurts now, the game he'd started backfiring as blood continued to fill his aching cock.

She tested his restraint like no other woman and he prayed he'd be able to keep his promise of not fucking her. For now. He had bigger plans for when he took her again. Plans that didn't include the possibility of interruption at any moment.

He teased his finger along the edge of her panties. "What will I find when I touch you, Jess?" He smiled against her neck as she tilted to give him better access. "That's my girl." He nipped the sensitive tissue at the base of her neck.

"You'll find me ready." Her voice was thick with need. "God, Garrett. Touch me, damn it."

* * *

Crazy. That's what he made her. Bat-shit, ready for the loony bin, crazy.

Jessa had never met a man who'd willingly admit to being celibate for a year, but then to admit sex with her had rattled him? She'd never left a man breathless before. She didn't know what to do with that. Garrett was straight-forward. Honest in a way that surprised the hell out of her. He didn't play around.

God, unless it was with her nipples.

She held his head as he passed from one breast to the other, leaving a wet trail of kisses between. Her skin tingled, tightened across muscles gone rigid with pleasure. Holy shit, the man knew what to do with his mouth.

Jessa had known she'd never get away with it. Secretly hoped she wouldn't. After last night, she didn't know how she'd ever manage to get Garrett Donovan out of her system. She'd been stupid to think she could avoid him.

He was her job, after all.

She was supposed to watch, not touch. No sweet, sweet touching.

His hands teased the edge of her panties until she was rolling her hips forward, silently begging him to move lower. Forget the idea of no touching. It was far too late for that. Far too late.

She threaded her fingers through his hair, lacing them together behind his head as he feasted on her breasts. Thank God he'd lifted her and wrapped her limbs around his hips because she was sure her legs had quit working. Her head and shoulders rode the wall as she savored the sensations coursing through her body. Sizzling sparks of fire that raced from her nipples to her womb as he nipped and sucked at her.

Releasing her breast, he moved upward, trailing his tongue over her collarbone and up her neck. Shivers racked her body as velvet lips caressed her cheek, drawing a path to her ear. Warm breath tickled her senses as his tongue traced the outer shell. "Have dinner with me. In my room."

One hand held her neck while the other skimmed to her waistline. He shifted his hips and opened her to his roaming hand. His fingers breached her panties, easing over her pussy, aching and wet with desire.

"Yes, Garrett. God, yes. I'll have dinner with you."

He traced her slit, light and teasing, before cradling her with his hand. "Not only tonight, Jessa."

"What? What are you … mmm." The needs of her body overrode basic brain function. She fought to track his words instead of the path of his finger, now circling her entrance. She met his gaze and knew instantly he'd get whatever he wanted from her. His heavy lids, the sensual curve of his mouth. Every part of him set her on fire, but it was the heat in his eyes that did it for her. Without a doubt, he wanted her. It was intoxicating, made her desperate to throw caution to the wind.

His thumb caressed her cheek as his other hand played havoc in her panties. "We still have over a week before you go back to New York. Spend it with me. The nights, I mean."

She dug her heels into his ass and rocked against his fingers, trying to force them inside her. "You know that's not a good idea. We can't get too involved. Too risky." She moaned the last part as he finally gave her what she wanted — his finger inside her, teasing the sensitive tissue deep within.

The irony of not getting involved was lost in the heat of the moment.

"We'll be careful."

He added another finger, then another, stretching her in that glorious way that made her nerve endings sing. "And what happens at the end of the week, Garrett?" she breathed. "We just walk away from each other?"

His response was buried against her lips as he overtook her mouth, squelching further conversation.

The breath left her lungs as he stroked in and out of her wet folds. His thumb pressed against her clit, making her feverish with the need to come. She rocked against him, rode his hand hard, until her entire body sizzled. She erupted, crying into his mouth as her release pounded through her system. She cupped his head, unwilling to give up his kiss as she drifted back to earth.

He broke away, resting his forehead against hers. He eased his fingers from her, bringing them to his mouth to lick them clean. "God, you taste like sunshine."

"Really, Garrett? What does sunshine taste like exactly?" Watching him lick her juices from his fingers stirred something inside her.

He smacked his lips as he finished with his fingers. A wicked smile crossed his face. "Like this," he said before claiming her mouth again.

She tasted herself on his tongue, a tangy mixture of her and Garrett all rolled into one. It was a flavor she could get used to, made her wonder how he'd react to kissing her mouth after he'd filled it. She'd find out, hopefully sooner rather than later.

With a final nip to her bottom lip, Garrett released her. His erection prodded her belly as her legs slid to the floor. She would have gone to her knees, but he pulled her up short.

"Later, sweetheart. That's not what I came up here for." He ran his thumbs over her nipples before nestling her breasts back into her bra and straightening her shirt. His chest expanded as he set to fastening her shorts. "It seems a shame to cover up such perfection."

Jessa burst out a laugh. "If you weren't so good at the plate, I'd think you'd need glasses."

"Nothin' wrong with my eyes."

"So, is this what you came up here for?"

He arched a brow and stepped away from her. Her legs wobbled before she found her footing.

"Honestly? I don't know. I was frustrated that I hadn't seen you all day and then that text message … well, needless to say I wasn't happy. All I could think about was getting to you so I could remind you how good it was between us." He grinned. "I may have considered spanking your ass as well."

"You wouldn't." Although her body warmed at the idea.

He wrapped his arms around her and kissed the top of her head. "It seems you bring out a side of me I've not dealt with before. So yeah, I most definitely would."

CHAPTER NINE

Feeling pleased with himself, Garrett was grinning like a loon as he made his way through the lobby. The smile was wearing out the muscles in his face, but damn if he could stop.

After leaving Jessa this afternoon, he'd actually managed to salvage his workout for the day. His coaches were happy and that meant he'd done his job. Couldn't ask for much more than that.

He'd chosen to rush back to the hotel instead of showering at the park. He was gritty with dried sweat and his muscles ached, but he'd never felt better. Now, if he could coax Jessa into the shower with him, he'd have his wicked way with her before they settled down for dinner, making the day damn near perfect.

He couldn't believe he'd admitted to wanting to spank her any more than her reaction to it. Her eyes had glazed over with desire. Oh yeah, she'd be into it. The thought had his mind wandering into all kinds of interesting territory. Jessa bent over his lap, her ass offered up like a sacrifice. Jessa tied to his bed, unable to do anything but accept the pleasure he wanted to give her. Fuck. Just what he needed. A massive hard-on in the middle of the hotel lobby.

He didn't know where his thoughts were coming from. These

weren't things he'd ever done, or even been tempted to do. But with Jessa, all bets were off. She brought out the side of him that wanted to possess her in every way possible.

"We just walk away from each other?"

The words floated through his mind and caused him to stumble.

"Easy there. What's up, buddy?" Tyler's arm clapped over his shoulders, steadying him, pulling him out of his reverie.

Garrett shrugged him off. "Tired, I guess. Wasn't watching where I was going."

Tyler held up the 12-pack of beer. "I've got just the thing. Come on."

"No thanks, I'm looking forward to a shower and hitting the sack early." With Jessa.

"Too late. I already told Jim and Miles to meet us in your room." Tyler gave him a knowing smile. "Hope you didn't have plans."

Bastard. Garrett ground his teeth, reminding himself that kicking Tyler's ass wouldn't be the best idea. At least not in front of all these people. "Then un-tell them. I'm tired. I'm surprised *you* don't have plans. You run out of ladies to torment already?"

Tyler snorted. "This city is swarming with women."

"So, why are you bothering me?" He waved his hands. "Go, get laid. Leave me alone."

Tyler stopped, one hand clutching the beer while he shoved the other in the front pocket of his jeans. "I'm only looking out for you."

Garrett sighed. "Yeah, Ty, I know. And I don't want to seem ungrateful, but you've got to back off me a bit. I'm not a kid and you're not responsible for me."

Tyler's lips thinned. He stared hard at him for a minute before nodding his head. "Don't fuck up. That's the last I'll say on the situation."

"Right. I'll believe that when I see it."

"We good?" Tyler's voice was weary, as if he knew this wasn't the end of it, but was willing to let it go.

Garrett smiled and extended his hand. "Stay away from my room and we're golden."

Tyler grasped his hand, pulling him forward until they bumped shoulders. "You got it. Watch yourself."

"Tyler."

"Okay, okay. I'm out. Later, brother."

Garrett entered his room and stopped short, his heart skipping a beat as he saw Jessa sitting on the couch, her knees drawn up to her chest. Her laptop was open on the table and he could hear sound coming from the TV.

He was pleased she'd used the key he'd given her earlier to let herself in. Even more so that she seemed to have made herself comfortable.

"Garrett, come here, come here." She waved him over, her eyes glued to the screen.

"What are you watching?"

"You. Check it out." She sat forward, her backside resting on the edge of the couch, her fingers flying over the keys of her computer as she looked from TV to laptop and back again.

He groaned and collapsed onto the couch next to her. He took the bottle of water she handed him and drank it down. "Thanks. Why are you watching this?" Garrett cringed at his face plastered on the sportscast.

She pointed at the screen. "Look how gorgeous you are. How could I not watch?" She tilted her head to the side, playfully offering him her mouth.

Well, wasn't this was a welcome change in behavior? Far be it for him to turn down an opportunity like that. He bent, tugging her pouty bottom lip into his mouth, caressing his tongue over the silky skin and swallowing her moan.

Her tongue darted across his lips before she pulled away, eyes narrowed. "You didn't shower at the park?"

He rolled, grabbing her waist, tickling her as he pulled her under him.

"Garrett!" Jessa kicked her legs with a fit of laughter. "Stop!"

"What's the matter, baby? You don't like sweaty men?"

She wrapped her legs around his waist and pulled him close. "Oh, I love sweaty men. The more the merrier I always say." Her eyes twinkled with amusement.

"Is that right?" He tickled her again, ignoring the stab of resentment that popped up at the thought of another man touching her.

She squirmed under him, the rich sound of her amusement music in his ears.

"Okay, okay! Uncle! You're the only sweaty man I love. I swear, I swear!"

Garrett froze, watching as a flush crept up her neck.

"I mean, you're the only sweaty man I want. Shit, you know what I mean! You can't hold me responsible for anything I say when you're tickling me." She swatted his ass. "Get off. Go shower and I'll take care of dinner."

Part of him wanted to forget hearing the *love* word come out of her mouth. Another part wanted to hear it again. He'd be ignoring that last part. "Come, shower with me." He pressed his nose into her neck, breathing in her scent. God, she always smelled so good. "I've been dying to get you wet all day."

Her lighthearted laugh warmed the center of his chest. He could definitely get used to that sound.

"Considering what happened earlier today, I'd say you accomplished your goal."

She pushed against him until he finally released her with a sigh. "I'm really dirty. Not sure I can reach all the places that need reaching."

Her eyes were back on the sportscast. "You'll have to manage. I've got to make a few more calls and then I'll order us something to eat. Anything in particular you're craving?"

He arched a brow, curling his lips as he looked at her breasts. Oh yeah, he had a craving. "I'd be happy to show you what I'd like to eat, darlin'."

"It's called time management, Garrett. If I get my work done while you shower, we'll have more time to …" She put her palms on his thigh and pushed herself up to plant a chaste kiss on his mouth, giving him an amazing view straight down her shirt in the process. He groaned. She wasn't wearing a bra. "… have dinner."

She was killing him. "You're a tease. Evil, wicked, tease."

She pecked his mouth again and moved away. "Protein. You need protein. Steak okay?"

He wasn't going to win. He hadn't known her long, but long enough to know she was back in business mode. He'd make sure she made it up to him later. "Yeah, steak is great. Medium rare, if you don't mind."

"Baked potato?"

"No, thanks, but a salad would be great."

She shook her head. "I'd never guessed you'd turn down potatoes for a salad. I figured a farm boy like you would be all about meat and potatoes."

He patted his stomach as his cell phone rang. "Gotta watch my figure." He put the phone to his ear. "Hey, Harlon." He mouthed a thank you to Jessa and hitched his thumb toward the bedroom.

She smiled and made a shooing motion at him, indicating he should go.

He looked back at her as he entered the bedroom. She was typing on her laptop again, taking frequent glances at the TV. A warm feeling spread through him. It was all so natural, her being here. It felt good. Right.

Oh boy.

The voice drifting through the phone got his attention. "Yeah, I'm here, man. What's up?"

* * *

Mortified. That was the only way to describe how Jessa felt. She'd said she loved him. Well, not *really*. Had she?

Shit.

She was getting in too deep. Her father would blow an artery if he found out what she'd been doing with his star player. And she'd be going back to New York soon. Sure, Garrett would be taking up residence there once the season started, but that didn't mean anything. None of it meant anything. They were passing time together. Very pleasurable time, but that was it. Nothing more.

Yeah, her heart wasn't buying it any more than her brain.

She needed to keep things light. Fun. As if they were friends. With benefits.

'Cause that never goes wrong.

It was over an hour before Garrett returned, his hair wet from the shower. His face was drawn, a furrow occupying the space between his brows.

"Everything all right?"

He nodded. "Yeah. It's just … my mom, ya know?"

No. She really didn't. Jessa didn't remember her mom. She'd seen pictures and heard the stories, but the only story that mattered was the one that ended with her mother leaving her husband and child without a word. "What about her?"

He shrugged. "Nothing earth shattering. She worries about things she shouldn't worry about. I thought when Leah and the baby moved in, it would help distract her, but she's still insistent about being involved with the farm. She doesn't know the first thing about what's going on."

"And she expects you to take care of it from here?" She took a seat at the table, motioning for him to do the same. The delicious scents coming from the steel covered plates made her mouth water.

He went to the refrigerator and pulled out a beer, holding up a bottle for her. "You want one?"

"Water, please."

He nodded once and ducked again to pull out a bottle of water.

"We have a foreman. He's a good man and he works hard. Hell, I leave him to look out for my family, so of course I trust him to run things. The fact is, I couldn't be here without him. I don't understand why — and it frustrates the hell out of me sometimes — but Mom won't use the money I've left without talking to me about every little detail." Sliding into the chair across from her, he twisted the cap off the water bottle before placing it in front of her. "She should be talking to him," he murmured.

"Hold on, what do you mean you couldn't be here without your foreman?"

"I meant what I said."

Yeah, Jessa was beginning to understand that about him.

Garrett lifted the lids off their plates and set them to the side. "Mmm, princess. This smells good enough to eat."

"Too bad I can't take credit for anything other than dialing the phone," she joked. "So, the farm is more important to you than playing baseball?" She handed him a napkin and he, in turn, passed her the silverware. The ease at which they moved through the motions of readying for dinner stunned her. It was as if they'd done this a hundred times. It was strangely intimate, intoxicating in its simplicity.

"My *family* is more important to me than playing baseball. The farm is all my mom has left of my dad and she loves it. She refuses to give it up. Actually, it would be a lot easier for all of us if they moved to New York with me, but Mom won't even consider leaving Mississippi. And Leah and the baby are better off staying with her there."

He cut a piece of his steak, his eyes rolling back in his head as he put it in his mouth. The muscles in his jaw bunched as he chewed, his throat working to swallow it down. "God, that's good." He washed it down with a swig of beer before turning his attention back to her.

"Farming is a tough business, princess. It's backbreaking, sun up to sundown work. Sometimes the yield is good, sometimes it's not. The times it's not can drive a man into the ground. Harlon manages the farm, which makes it possible for me to play baseball. Baseball ensures we keep the farm. See how it all works?" He grinned and took a large bite of his salad.

She did. She understood how important playing ball was, not only to Garrett, but to his family as well. They relied on him. He'd used the money he earned to make sure his mom kept her beloved farm, and he'd kept his father's memory alive. He took care of his sister and now, her daughter as well. What would it feel like to be on the receiving end of a love like that?

Her heart lurched as she realized their playing around could hurt a lot of people. People Garrett was devoted too, people he loved. She knew he'd sacrifice himself for the good of his family. He'd be an outstanding husband and father, one day.

Lucky was the woman who would call him hers. "It's good of you to look out for them."

He shook his head, dismissing her compliment. "I'm doing what any other man would do."

"That's where you're wrong. There are a lot of men — men older than you — who wouldn't go to such lengths to make sure their families were cared for."

"Then they aren't men." Disgust marred his features. "Doesn't matter anyway. I take care of my own. Always have, always will. Whether it's the cotton field or the ball field." He winked at her and motioned to her plate. "Eat up before it gets cold."

She should walk away. Stop this now before anyone gets hurt. It was the right thing to do. But the devil would reserve a special place for her in hell because she wasn't strong enough. It was selfish and greedy, but she couldn't let him go. Not yet.

Overwhelmed with the need to touch him, Jessa put down her silverware and moved around the table. Before he could move, she straddled his lap and wrapped her arms around his neck in a tight hug. He spent all his time taking care of other people, who took care of him? Who did he talk to when things got tough? Did he have anyone to lean on?

Jessa wanted to be that person. Even if it was only for a short time.

"What's this?" Laughter tinged his voice and she heard his fork drop a second before he enclosed her within his arms.

She reveled in the warmth of his skin against her face. So alive, so vibrant and strong. She needed every inch of his body touching hers. To pretend, for one moment, that they could be more than a passing fling. That they could see where this attraction between them would lead. She tugged on his T-shirt, arching away from him to remove it.

"Princess?" He released her long enough to raise his arms so she could finish what she'd started.

Her eyes teared up as she tossed his shirt aside and ran her palms over his chest.

He pinched her chin, forcing her to look at him. "Hey, now.

What's going on in that head of yours?"

She was being a silly, hormonal girl. She swiped at her eyes and laughed. "I have this uncontrollable desire to get you naked."

"I'm all for getting naked." His large hands enclosed her wrists, staying her. "But why the tears, Jess?"

"I don't know, Garrett," she lied, not wanting to ruin the moment. "I just want to be with you."

CHAPTER TEN

There was no way he could deny her. Not when she looked at him like that. Her beautiful blue eyes glistening with unshed tears he didn't understand.

God save him from a woman's tears. It was the one thing guaranteed to have him in knots, desperate to either run or, in Jessa's case, soothe her sadness into something much more pleasurable.

Garrett switched hands, holding her wrists in one while cupping the back of her neck with the other. Her skin was hot, her cheeks flushed a pretty pink. He moved his fingers into her hair, the silky strands teasing him with their softness. Unable to control the urge to taste her, he tightened his grip and pressed his lips to hers.

He loved that she opened without so much as a nudge on his part. She offered her mouth much like she'd offered her body, trusting him to take her where she needed to go.

She moaned into his kiss as her nails dug into his biceps, as if she needed to attach herself to him.

"Take your shirt off, baby," he mumbled between kisses, moving from her mouth to her ear.

She shivered as he suckled her lobe, teasing the sensitive skin until she squirmed on his lap. He released her wrists and eased her back. "Now, Jess." His voice rasped with need as his cock swelled to a painful degree.

She stripped the garment over her head and tossed it in the general direction she'd sent his shirt flying.

He stood, lifting her with him. His hands gripped her ass, his fingers so close to the intimate folds of her pussy, her heat burned him.

"Don't make me wait, Garrett. Here. Now."

The sadness he'd seen in her eyes vanished, replaced by a need he was sure matched his own. He carried her to the end of the table and placed her on the edge, away from their dinner.

"You sure you want to do this here?" He hooked his thumbs in the waistband of his shorts.

"No waiting. Not even to get to the bedroom."

His cock throbbed, mirroring her impatience. He jutted his chin. "The shorts and panties have to go. I want to see every beautiful inch of you."

He heard her slight intake of breath a moment before she lifted her hips and shimmied her shorts off her hips.

Within seconds, Jessa was naked and Garrett was a goner.

She was spread out like a feast to his senses. The delicate scent of her skin, mixed with her arousal, made his head spin. The sight of her breasts, heaving as she fought for breath, nipples darkened and drawn tight, had his mouth watering. He rolled his tongue in anticipation.

"I'm not big on sweets, but what I wouldn't give for some whipped cream right now. Guess I'll have to improvise." He reached around and ran his fingers across his plate, coating them with the juice from his steak.

Jessa moaned, watching as he spread the liquid around tip of her breast. He closed his lips around the bud and sucked hard.

Delicious.

"Now, Garrett." Her nails bit into his shoulders as she raised her hips. "Fuck me now."

Garrett cursed and pulled away. "Don't move."

He bit back a smile as she let her head drop back to the table with a thud. He reached for the condom he'd put in his pocket after his shower.

"No, Garrett. Don't," Jessa panted, raising her head to look at him. "I don't want anything between us. Just you and me, remember? I want to feel you. For you to feel me." She let her head drop back to the table. "We're safe, we're protected. Garrett, please."

Garrett groaned at the thought of taking her bare. Her heat drawing him, sinking into his skin. "Okay, Jessa." He ran his hands up the inside of her thighs, loving the feel of her silky smooth skin against his. "Show me whatcha got."

He gripped the base of his cock, rubbing it through her slick heat before easing the tip inside her. Damn, she was tight. Tight enough to make a man lose his mind.

Her back arched as he pushed forward, his hands spread wide across her hips. "Fuck, Jess. You're so hot. You make me want to forget to be gentle. To go slow."

She raised her head to look at him. "So don't. I won't break, I promise. Fuck me, Garrett. Please …"

He surged forward, not waiting for her to adjust to his size before burying himself to the hilt. Her pussy seized, clutching at him as the warmth of her arousal bathed his length and stole his breath.

She cried out, her hands reaching out to grip the edge of the table. Her skin was flushed, glistening with perspiration.

"Jesus, you're so wet. Do you know how good you feel wrapped around my cock?" Garrett eased back, mesmerized by the sight of her sex as it opened for him.

She smiled. A slow, sensual smile. She tightened her inner muscles, her fist-tight grip clenching him.

"Fuck!" He growled before he slammed into her again. Pleasure rocked his system as he grabbed her shoulders, anchoring himself to her as he moved. Back and forth. In and out.

He couldn't think beyond the need. Need that was tearing through his veins like a runaway freight train.

Jessa cried out as she shifted her hips and he gained deeper access. He fought for breath as he fought his release.

Her first. He had to make sure it was as good for her as it was for him. And Christ, it was so fucking good.

Garrett tightened his grip on her shoulders and thrust hard, powering in and out of her until sweat trickled from his temples.

Ah, hell. The heated grip of her pussy was driving him insane. He wasn't going to last.

"Can't hold off much longer, Jessa. So hot. God, so fucking hot."

He reached between them. "Come, baby. Come, now." He flicked his thumb back and forth, teasing her sensitive nub.

Jessa screamed, her back arching off the table, pushing him deeper into her rippling flesh. The force of her orgasm almost bringing him to his knees.

It was more than he could take. Pleasure swamped him, surging through his body and exploding in a million fragments. He slammed into her, shouting with his release as her body continued to contract around him.

His hips jerked as she continued to milk his seed. He couldn't see straight. His legs were shaking so badly, he was afraid he'd fall over and make a fool of himself.

Garrett wrapped his arms around Jessa and pulled her close, kissing the top of her hair as he struggled for air. Still buried inside her, he eased back into a chair. She wrapped around him like a monkey and snuggled into his chest with a sigh.

Wanting to enjoy the feel of her for a little longer, Garrett ignored his shaky limbs and held her tight. He also ignored the desire to keep her wrapped around him for more than tonight. For more than this week. This month.

They were fucking. Having a good time. That was it. At the end of the week it'd be over and his life would go back to normal.

Normal sucked.

* * *

Every bone in her body had liquefied.

And Garrett had the most comfortable lap she'd ever curled up in. Granted, she didn't make a habit of curling up in men's laps, but she was sure Garrett's would win, hands down.

Which made it that much harder to move.

"We can't stay like this all night." Garrett's voice rumbled against her cheek.

Spoil sport. "One more minute. I think all my limbs are broken."

He chuckled. "I'm gonna take that as a compliment."

She pushed off him, a chill shaking her body at the loss of his heat. "You should."

"Then I return the compliment, princess, because I don't think my legs are gonna work either."

She stretched her hands out. "Come on, hotshot, let's get cleaned up and finish dinner. I'm starving."

He groaned, but let her pull him to his feet.

She shrieked as he scooped her up, carrying her through the bedroom and into the bathroom. It wasn't quite as large as hers, but it was still a nice sized suite with all the amenities.

He placed her on the counter, the marble cool against the bare skin of her backside. He methodically set about warming a cloth and she hissed as he pressed it between her legs.

He jerked away. "Too hot?"

"No, no. It's okay." Weird. She wasn't used to being cared for like this. It was awkward, but she allowed him to press her knees farther apart. His brow creased as he wiped the warm rag over her swollen flesh.

It was touching, his gentle ministrations. A vast difference from the man who had fucked her silly a few minutes ago.

She cleared her throat. "I'm curious about something."

"I'm an open book, darlin'. Have at it."

Her body tightened at the image his words brought to mind. Garrett sprawled naked on the bed, his cock hard and ready for her to taste and enjoy. Jeez, she was acting like a horny teenager.

She cleared her throat, trying to sound nonchalant so he wouldn't guess her real motive. "Why aren't you sharing a room with Tyler? You guys are friends. Why the suite by yourself?"

He gave her a droll stare. "You mean did I pay for my own room because I was planning to hook up with someone?"

Busted.

"If you want to know something, Jessa, ask." He leaned in and kissed her forehead.

She scowled at him. "Okay, fine. Did you get your own room in case you hooked up with someone?"

"No." He turned, giving her a spectacular view of his naked ass as he walked away.

She hopped off the counter and followed him into the bedroom. "That's all I get?"

Garrett pulled on a pair of shorts, covering up all that male hotness. Damn, but the man had an endless supply. Of shorts and hotness.

"What more do you want me to say? No, I didn't get this suite for a hook up." He considered her. "Although, it's a damn good thing I did, don't you think?"

"Very funny."

He crossed his arms, his brow cocked arrogantly as he glanced over her naked body. "If you want to continue to talk, I'd suggest clothes. Stat. Otherwise … well … here."

He tossed her a T-shirt and she pulled it over her head.

The material was soft with age, a subtle male spice lingering in the fibers. She wanted to cover her nose and breathe it in. It felt strange wearing his shirt. Possessive. Not something she should feel about Garrett.

At least it fell to her knees, covering any part of her that may entice him.

"Jesus, you look sexy as fuck in my shirt, princess."

Or not.

"The suite," she prompted.

"I roomed with Tyler all through college. Why would I want to put myself through that mess again?"

She narrowed her eyes at his back as he, yet again, left her to follow him as he moved from the room. "What aren't you telling me?"

He snorted as he sat on the couch, stretching his legs out in front of him and folding his hands over his stomach. "Still think I'm the spoiled athlete who needs a babysitter, Jessa? Apparently, you have your players mixed up. I got this suite because I like peace and quiet. I like my privacy. Two things that are impossible to achieve when Tyler is around. I need to focus on my game and not worry about walking in on him having sex in my living room."

"So, instead of focusing on your game, *you're* the one having sex in the living room. With me."

"That's not what I meant."

"It's all right. I get it."

"You get what, Jess?" He sat forward, irritation etched on his face. "You asked me a question and I answered it. Don't make it something it's not. You aren't distracting me from anything." He put a hand up to stop her from speaking. "I can see it all over your face, so don't deny it."

"How can I not feel like I'm a distraction, Garrett?" Her own irritation with the situation boiled to the surface. "You said yourself you didn't plan to hook up and you need to focus. Well, guess what? You hooked up and you're not focusing. Both because of me."

"I'm not focusing?" His tone was filled with disbelief. "Last I checked, princess, my game is solid. I had one lousy batting practice. Won't be my last. Stop making excuses. Do you want to be here with me or not?"

How in the hell was she supposed to answer that? They were in a no-win situation. A no-win for him. All she risked was her dad's wrath, which would pass over time. Garrett was risking his job and his reputation. "It's not fair to you."

He ran his fingers through his hair, letting his head linger in his hands a moment before looking at her again. "What happened?"

"What?"

"Between the incredible sex we had and right now. What happened? Because I'm lost."

"Of course I want to be with you, otherwise I wouldn't be here. But I didn't consider the consequences. And if we get caught, there will be consequences, Garrett. I'm not worth all the trouble this could cause you."

For the first time in her life, Jessa wished she was someone else. An average woman with an average father. It seemed no matter what she did, who she was always came back to bite her on the ass.

"Bullshit. I don't want to hear talk like that from you. You're worth fifty of me, all day and twice on Sunday. If we get caught, and that's a big if, I'll deal with the consequences."

"You make it sound so easy."

"I won't lie to you, Jess. I've considered the ramifications of this thing between us, and none of them are good."

"And you don't care about that?"

"Of course I do. Christ, Jessa, the last thing I need is to piss off your dad."

"Exactly. We need to quit while we're ahead. Back to business."

Garrett nodded, his gaze focused on the table in front of him. His voice was soft when he finally spoke. "We still have a few days."

Was he insane? Didn't he realize he was prolonging the inevitable? "But —"

"No. No, buts. I like you, Jessa. I like spending time with you and I *really* like having sex with you. I assume you feel the same, so why deny ourselves the pleasure of each other's company for a few more days?"

"Have you not been listening?"

"I'm a big boy, I can make my own decisions. Let me worry about it." He sighed. "And this topic of conversation is over."

She studied the rigid line of his jaw and she knew he'd won. He wouldn't give up and she didn't want to resist. God forbid, if they got caught. But if they did, she'd make damn sure Garrett wasn't blamed. He would not pay for her selfishness.

Her mind made up, Jessa couldn't do more than nod. "I'd better get back to my room. I don't want to take a chance that someone sees me leaving at an inappropriate hour." She tried to smile. "And wearing your T-shirt."

"You're not staying?" He checked the time. "I'd hardly say eight o'clock is an inappropriate hour."

"No, but any later would be hard to explain. It's best if I go now."

He stiffened, obviously unhappy with her answer. "What about dinner?"

"I'm not hungry anymore."

"Jessa. You're over-thinking this. It's not as though we're having sex where anyone can see us."

She gave him a hard look.

"Okay." He stood and wrapped his arms around her. "This afternoon at the ballpark notwithstanding. I promise to be more discreet. No handholding, no secret touches, and definitely no ass grabbing unless we're alone in this room. Come on, princess. We're safe here." He pressed his mouth to her ear. "You know you wanna," he whispered.

"Your charm won't work on me."

"No?" His boyish grin had her biting back her own.

"No." His grin morphed into a full-on smile and it was obvious he didn't believe her. With good reason. He probably got everything he wanted by flashing that handsome smile of his. Yeah, she was done for.

She poked him hard in the chest. "If your game slips, I'll kick your ass."

"Yes, ma'am."

"And I'm still not staying the night." She raised up and gave him a quick kiss. "Goodnight, Garrett."

CHAPTER ELEVEN

"Jessa, I've been looking all over for you."

Jessa looked up from her laptop, blinking a few times to focus on the cute little redhead standing in the doorway.

"Amy!" Jessa couldn't hide her surprise. "It's good to see you." Jessa waved her in. "I had a really great time at dinner the other night. I've been meaning to call you to say thanks for letting me crash the party."

Amy was about as sweet and real as they came. She'd treated Jessa like a long lost sister, something Jessa wouldn't forget. For the first time in longer than she could remember, she'd tasted genuine friendship from a woman who didn't see her as anything but herself. Plain ole Jessa.

It was refreshing.

But it didn't explain why Amy had sought her out. Or why she was out of breath. "Not that I'm not happy to see you, but what are you doing down here? Are you okay?"

Amy put her palm to her chest and drew in a deep breath. "I think the better question is, what are *you* doing down here? I mean, really, Jessa." Amy scrunched up her perk little nose. "It smells like wet socks."

Jessa laughed and looked around the cramped little office. Not an office so much as a closet with a desk and a couple of chairs. There were no personal items scattered about, no file cabinets or any other items that would make this anything other than a space for the transient. It was buried in the catacombs of the stadium, but it was quiet and empty. Two things she'd needed in order to catch up on the work she'd neglected while "watching" Garrett.

"Take a seat before you have a heart attack. Did you run all the way down here?"

"No, of course not." Amy slid into the chair, concern etched on her face. "I ran all *over* down here. Well, walked actually, and I'm feeling very out of shape. I didn't realize how many places there are to hide around here."

Jessa thought about that. "I guess it would be easy to get lost if you didn't know where you were going. And I'm not hiding." She motioned to the papers spread across the desk. "I'm working."

Amy waved her off. "Well, there are a lot of places to work around here then, too. Who knew this place was so big!"

"I grew up in stadiums like this, so I guess you could say I'm used to it."

"Your father is rather hands-on, isn't he? Not that I'm complaining, mind you. Miles loves playing for this team."

Jessa smiled. It wasn't the first time she'd been asked that question and it wouldn't be the last. A lot of people thought it was strange, the amount of time TJ Montgomery spent with his beloved team. Some even criticized that he was a micro-manager, not able to give control to his coaches and managers. It was bullshit, but Jessa figured their record of four World Series wins in the last eight years could speak for itself.

TJ took an active interest in his players, not as a coach or a boss, but as a mentor and friend. He left the coaching to the coaches, the managing to the managers. Instead, he'd counseled on everything from dating and marriage proposals to children and the best school systems. He was there for them. Right or wrong, TJ considered the men family. Sons.

"He loves the game. He wanted me to love it too, I suppose, so he always brought me along. While tutors schooled me in math and science, Dad taught me everything there was to know about baseball." She chuckled. "I always thought he'd wished I'd been a boy. Sometimes, I get a little sensitive about it."

"I'm sure that's not true. Your father must love you very much to include you in his life in such a way."

Jessa shrugged. She knew her dad loved her. It had never been a question of that.

"Besides," Amy continued, "he's got all the boys he needs right out there and he doesn't have to worry about them eating him out of house and home, smelling up the place with sweaty gym clothes, or burping at the dinner table. It's the best of both worlds."

Jessa really liked this woman.

"Ugh, forget about my dad. You've made me grateful for my breasts."

Amy snickered and shot her a wink. "It's always good to have perspective. I did search you out to say hi and visit for a bit, but truth be known, the real reason I came to find you was to let you know one of the players was hurt on — "

"Is Garrett all right?" Jessa's heart jumped as cold dread filled her system.

"— the field." Amy finished over her interruption. Blue eyes narrowed in scrutiny.

"Garrett's fine," Amy said slowly. "It's Tyler."

Jessa cursed and squirmed under Amy's intense stare. She could feel the woman reading her thoughts until all of her secrets were laid bare. Her only hope was that Amy would let it go.

"Tyler? What happened?" Please, please let it go.

"I'm not sure the extent. Shoot, I'm not exactly sure what happened." Her cheeks blushed deep enough to match her hair. "I was goofing around on my phone and wasn't watching. I did see him walk off the field, but his arm was curled into his chest. I figured since you were here, you'd want to know."

"Shit. I should probably get over there."

Jessa stood and started collecting her papers, shoving them into her bag with more force than necessary, chastising herself for her own stupidity. She hadn't anticipated how hard it would be to act normal about her relationship with Garrett. She needed to be more careful.

"There's no need to hurry. Tyler will more than likely be with the doctors. Nothing you can do for him right now, so you can stay and talk to me about what's going on with you and Garrett." Amy grinned knowingly.

Jessa fought to keep her expression calm. "What do you mean?"

"Oh, come on. I was there the other night. It was obvious he wasn't happy about you dancing with Tyler. And girl, the way he took hold of you on that dance floor had me ready to jump my own husband."

"I ... I didn't realize." Jessa felt her cheeks burn.

"Honey, anyone with eyes could see that boy has it bad for you."

Panic began to set in. "Oh, no. No, it's not like that at all, Amy. We're hanging out. Dad sent me here to keep an eye on him. I'm doing my job."

"That's some job description." Amy's laugh was loud and boisterous. "Oh, don't look so worried, Jessa. Your secret is safe with me."

* * *

"Ow!"

Garrett watched from the doorway as the doctor worked to stabilize Tyler's shoulder. Tyler's face was flushed, his eyes burning a hole through Garrett's forehead. Garrett offered him a hint of a smile, a showing of support his friend so obviously needed.

Garrett winced in sympathy as the next line of expletives burned his ears.

"What are you trying to do, Doc? Rip my damn arm off?"

Unaffected by his gruff, the doctor helped Tyler out of his jersey. "Looks like you did a good job of that yourself, Tyler." The good doctor smiled. "Without any help from me."

With speed and efficiency, the doctor wrapped a stabilizer around Tyler's chest and shoulder, tightening the Velcro straps around his arm. Seeming satisfied no further damage could be done, Dr. Adlyn stepped away from his patient and turned to Garrett. "There's a lesson to be learned in all this."

Tyler snorted. "Oh, please. Enlighten us, o' wise one."

Garrett chuckled. Dr. Adlyn was a relatively young and good-looking man. Garrett guessed he wasn't much into his forties and was one of the greatest damn orthopedic doctors in the country. As hands go, Tyler was in the best.

Dr. Adlyn smirked and shook his head. "Obviously, the pain meds haven't kicked in, so he's a bit grumpy."

"You think?" Tyler snapped, sitting on an examination table, swinging his feet like a three year old who needed to pee. The tension radiating from him was pliable, the sense of foreboding thick in the air. This couldn't be good.

Garrett gave up the safety of doorway and walked into the room. "Give the doc a break, Ty. He's only trying to help."

Dr. Adlyn clapped Garrett on the shoulder. "See that he doesn't hurt himself further until I get back. I've got to go make some arrangements for our friend here." He headed toward the door. "Save the heroics for when it counts, boys. That's the lesson here."

Garrett couldn't argue with the doc's parting shot. Tyler had been careless. Not paying attention. Distracted.

It could've been me.

Garrett hadn't been paying attention either. Hell, he hadn't even seen what happened, his thoughts being centered on the woman who was changing his world and all. Garrett had only been a few yards away, yet couldn't give an accurate account of how Tyler got hurt other than to generalize. Ball hit high toward the first base stands. It should've been a routine play.

Only now, this play would make the lead story on every sports channel highlight reel tonight.

Garrett had been the one distracted.

Several times last night he'd reached out, searching, wishing he'd find Jessa there. Wanting to curl into her delicious body and lose himself in her heat.

But she hadn't been there. All he'd had was the lingering scent of her skin on his sheets. A scent that made finding sleep hard and his dick harder.

He clenched his fists at the memory, shoving it deep into the recesses of his brain. This was not how he'd imagined things to go. He was here to play ball. That's it.

He'd do well to remember it, too.

Sighing, Garrett crossed his arms over his chest and looked at Tyler. "Well? What's the verdict?"

Tyler snorted. "Rotator cuff."

Garrett grimaced, understanding the ramifications of that kind of injury. "Sorry, man."

Tyler shrugged, then let out a groan. "Damn it. Don't make me move."

Garrett stifled a laugh. As if he could make Tyler do anything. "How bad is it?"

"Pretty fucking bad. Hurts like a screamin' motherfucker too. A foul ball. Jesus, it's pre-season. I should have let the fucker go. Better yet, I should have taken that tee time and been on the goddamn golf course while you rookies played warm-up. The doc says it's gonna need surgery, so it looks like I'm out for the season." Tyler cursed again under his breath. "I've never had a summer off. Guess I'm gonna see how the other half lives."

"It's lucky you weren't hurt worse, I guess." Garrett was at a loss as to what else to say.

"Yeah, I feel pretty fuckin' lucky right now. Like a fuckin' leprechaun."

It was clear by the amount of cussing that Tyler was none too happy about it, but hell, Garrett didn't blame him. Like himself, Tyler was a dedicated athlete who loved his sport. Garrett would go nuts if he had to watch from the sidelines, even if it were a game or two. Sitting out a whole season? Yeah, he felt for his friend.

Tyler's injury struck a chord. What if it *had* been him? Sure, Garrett had a healthy bank account now, but how long would that money last if he couldn't play ball? What the hell would he do with himself then? All it took was one injury to end a career.

Or fucking the owner's daughter.

He had responsibilities, people he'd let down if he fucked this up. Something he was well on his way to doing if he wasn't careful.

Shaking off his train of thought, Garrett focused on the more urgent matter at hand. "What's the plan?"

"I'm headin' home to Arkansas after surgery. Might as well recoup somewhere comfortable and quiet. Doc also said I'd be in physical therapy for up to twelve weeks. Maybe longer. Damn, this sucks."

Finding himself antsy, Garrett moved around the room, inspecting the equipment, checking the contents of containers.

"You look like shit."

Tyler's statement stopped him dead. "This, coming from the guy on the exam table."

"Seriously, Garrett. You look like you haven't slept in a week. Jessa keeping you up nights?"

"We're having a good time. You know? Playing around." Garrett turned and leaned his ass against the counter. They were doing more than playing around, but until he knew what that meant, he'd keep the information to himself. "No big deal."

Tyler nodded with feigned understanding. "Right," he drawled. "See, here's the thing, Garrett. Women like Jessa ... they don't play around. I don't care what she says. If y'all are having sex, she's given a piece of herself to you." He shifted his ass on the table and sucked in a breath. "It might be a tiny piece, but it's a piece none the same."

"When did you become Doctor-fucking-Phil? You, the man who's made fucking an Olympic sport. What do you know about how women feel?"

Tyler stared him dead in the eye. "It's a fact, brother. When this thing ends — and you know it will end — you'll take a piece of her with you. You'll know it. She'll know it. It'll change both of you. What then, G?" Tyler made a disgusted noise. "You're a fool if you think you'll walk away from this unscathed. Either of you. I never thought you were the kind of man to play with a woman like that."

"Who says I'm playing?" he barked before he could stop himself. "Maybe it doesn't have to end."

And there it was.

The thing that had been nagging Garrett all day.

He liked Jessa. She was beautiful and sweet. When she looked at him, he didn't feel like she was sizing up his cock, or his wallet. She saw beyond the hype to the man that he was underneath. That had to count for something.

"I know you and TJ are buddies, Garrett, but Jessa ... man, Jessa is his only daughter. How sure are you that he'd simply roll over and accept that you'd been fucking her?"

Not sure at all.

"Enough, Ty." Garrett growled. "We're done talking about this."

"Kiss my ass, Donovan. I'm the one with a fucking pack strapped around my shoulder. One stupid mistake and as far as this season is concerned, I'm done. But you're not. Your career is just getting started and here you are, bound and determined to make a mess of it. Jesus Christ, Garrett. Think about what you're doing. You'll lose credibility; your reputation would be shot. You'll be branded. Or worse."

Garrett tore his cap off his head and slapped it against his thigh. He shoved his other hand through his hair, ready to spit nails. "You think I don't know that?"

"I think you aren't thinking with the right head. You're letting your dick get in the way of your future."

What if Jessa is my future?

He pushed back the thought. "I thought you said you were done giving me shit about this."

"Yeah, well. I lied."

The fight drained out of him. "So it seems."

Tyler moved over and Garrett slid onto the exam table next to him.

"Do you love her?"

Surprised by his question, Garrett shook his head. "Of course not. It's too soon for all that." He waved his hand, dismissing the idea. "It's safe to say I like her, though."

Tyler considered him. "Man, you've got it bad."

Garrett pinched the bridge of his nose. "Yeah, man. I think I do.

Which means, either way, I'm fucked."

"Fucked about what?"

Garrett jumped off the table as Jessa walked into the room.

"Amy came and found me." She spared him a wary glance before moving closer to Tyler. "You okay?"

Tyler turned on the charm, causing Garrett to grit his teeth. "I'll live darlin', but I wouldn't say no to a little TLC."

Jessa's gaze darted his way before she smiled back at Tyler. "I'm sure you'll have the nurses lining up to take care of you. Don't worry." She patted him on the leg. "I've talked to the doctor. You'll be on your way in no time, and you'll be back next season good as new."

Garrett stood back, giving Jessa and Tyler time to talk about logistics. The sound of her voice lulled him. Admitting he liked her to Tyler had lifted a weight from his chest. As if those words alone were enough to chart a new course. As if it erased the obstacles that stood between them.

"Garrett? Can I see you outside for a second?"

"Sure, Jess." He gave Tyler a look that said he had no idea what she wanted and followed her out of the room. He pulled the door closed behind him. "You look good enough to eat," he teased once they were alone in the hallway.

"Garrett, stop."

"What? It's the truth. What I wouldn't give to pull you into one of the storage closets, pull down those jeans and —"

"No," she raised her palm to cut him off. "Amy knows, Garrett. If we keep this up, it won't be long before word gets back to my dad."

Garrett had a feeling he wouldn't like what was coming. "What are you saying, princess?"

"I'm saying we can't do this anymore. It's over. We have to stop."

Nope. He didn't like it one bit.

CHAPTER TWELVE

Three days later, Garrett sat back in the limo, his mood in the toilet.

The coaches were kicking his ass and he couldn't remember when his body had ever been so sore. Hell, even his hair hurt. He'd never felt more like a rookie in his life. He was determined to keep pace, to not let the seasoned professionals light his ass up like they did the other rookies. So far, he'd more than proved himself on the field. He'd worked hard for it. But his body was paying the price. All he wanted to do was take a shower and fall into bed.

Neither of which he wanted to do alone.

That led to his next problem: Jessa and her insane need to keep her distance. He glanced across the seat, her profile pensive as she stared out the window. Her jaw set in a firm line, making Garrett wonder if she ached like he did. Not that she'd share if she did. She hadn't shared anything with him these last few days except this incessant ego-mobile. Not a meal, hardly a look, and most definitely not his bed.

All business.

It was pissing him off. As if what they'd done was a dirty

little secret she needed to wipe under the carpet, even though he understood the need for secrecy was, for the most part, to protect him.

One more thing for him to feel like shit about.

She'd ended it with him because Amy knew. He chuckled to himself. If he'd told her Tyler also knew, she'd be on the first plane back to New York. He didn't know which was worse. Having her in his bed knowing it was temporary or not having her there at all.

Either way, Garrett hadn't been ready to end things between them.

Quite the opposite, in fact.

He wanted more. He wanted to feel her next to him as they slept. He wanted to wake up with her, to sink into her heat and fuck her as the sun came up. He wanted —

"Garrett?"

— things he shouldn't want.

Jessa's face was etched with concern. "You okay?"

He stared across the seat at her. "I'd be better if we were in a regular car," he grumbled, his piss-poor attitude latching on to whatever it could to feed itself. The guys on the team had stopped giving him grief about his luxury mode of transport, but in his present mood it didn't matter. It irked the shit out of him.

Her eyes narrowed. "What's up with you?"

"I'm sick of being schlepped around like a fucking movie star."

Jessa's lips thinned. "Okay."

He snorted. "Okay? That's it?"

She folded her hands in her lap. Her chest expanded as she drew in a deep breath, then let it out slowly. "Are you looking for a fight, Garrett? Because if you are, I'm not your girl."

"No," he snapped. "You're not my girl." He regretted the words the minute they'd vomited from his mouth. God, what was wrong with him? Maybe he should add a drink or two to his shower and bed plan.

He let his head fall back against the seat. He wasn't fit to keep company with a pack of wild dogs right now. Let alone the woman he wanted nothing more than to seduce.

Jessa turned to stare out the window. "I'm sorry you've had a hard day," she murmured.

Garrett clamped his lips shut, not responding for fear of saying something else he'd be sorry for.

Silence hung heavy for the rest of the ride to the hotel.

When they arrived, Garrett motioned for Jessa to exit before he followed her onto the sidewalk. They stood, facing each other in awkward silence, and Garrett felt a fist wrap around his heart.

She cleared her throat. "I guess I'll see you later. I'm going up."

He wanted to pull her into his arms and smooth away the sadness that shone in her eyes. Before he did something stupid, he jammed his hands into his pockets.

"Night, Jess," he said as she turned and disappeared into the hotel.

In the past, Garrett would limit the amount of alcohol he consumed during training, but tonight called for a revised schedule. He didn't have to report tomorrow — thank God — so tonight, he planned to get as drunk as possible.

To that end, he went to his room and made a beeline for his not-so-mini-bar. He bypassed the heavy stuff and grabbed a beer, popping the top and pouring it down his throat as fast as he could swallow. The cool liquid soothed his throat, but did nothing for his tired, aching body.

There was only one thing that would help him with that.

He should go up there. Barge into her room and remind her how he could make her scream. His dick sprang to life at the memory of the sweet sounds she made.

She'd been shy at first, unsure of herself as a woman. Until he'd shown her how much she turned him on, how much he wanted her.

He imagined knocking on her door. She'd open it, her mouth partially open with surprise. He wouldn't give her time to think. Thinking is what got them into this mess to begin with.

No thinking. He'd take her right there, right inside the door. He'd make her come before moving her to the couch, bending her over the edge, slamming into her from behind where he'd make them both come.

Fuck.

He gripped the edge of the bar, both hands turning white with effort. What was the matter with him? He'd never acted like this before. Focus. That was his game. And he was good at it. When he was on the field, nothing else existed. So why couldn't he get one tiny woman out of his head?

He needed another drink. He reached, hesitating a moment over the bottle of scotch on the counter. Tempting, but he'd rather have a slight headache than feel like he'd been run over by a truck. He'd stick with the beer.

Moving to the couch, he picked up the remote and turned on the TV. He moved through the channels as if on autopilot, not really caring what he landed on. He propped his legs on the table and rubbed his thighs.

Damn, he was sore. Sitting still was probably the last thing he should to do right now.

And he was still hard.

His phone rang and he cursed when he saw the number. He contemplated not answering. Yeah, after the little fantasy train he'd been ridin', that wasn't going to happen.

He drew in a deep breath, not wanting to snap at her again. "Hey, Jess."

"Garrett." Her voice was soft in his ear. "I need your help. Could you come up here, please?"

Garrett drained the second beer as she waited for his answer. He didn't trust himself to be around her. Not in this mood, and not with the wood he was currently sporting. He swiped a hand across his mouth. "I'm not fit for company tonight, Jess. Can't it wait?"

"No, Garrett, it can't. It'll only take a second."

That voice, so demanding and sexy. It was impossible to resist. Just because he was grouchy, didn't mean she should have to put up with it. He had self-control, damn it. "I'll be right there."

The stairs offered him the means to stretch his already stiffening muscles, as well as allowing him time to get a handle on his libido. It wouldn't do either of them any good to have him show up with an erection. He reviewed hand signals as he went, counted the steps, anything to get his mind off how Jessa felt when she was under him.

By the time he reached her room, he'd cooled enough to not embarrass himself.

Jessa opened the door and Garrett sucked air through his teeth. Her hair was piled on top of her head, exposing the long line of her neck. He ached to touch the escaping tendrils that framed her face.

Her black silk robe showed off her long legs. One flick of his wrist and that flimsy belt would fall open. Damn. Whatever she needed, she better be quick about it or he'd be hard pressed to keep his hands to himself.

A shy smile spread her lips. "Thanks for coming."

He shrugged in an attempt to act nonchalant as he moved past her into the suite. The scent of vanilla hung in the air. The soft light from the candles basked the room in a sultry glow. His erection surged back, in full, painful force.

"What's all this?" Warm fingers entwined with his and he turned to face her. "Jess?"

"Come with me." The low timbre of her voice lulled him, drew him in. She was his fantasy come true.

She pulled him toward the bedroom. His cock twitched, anticipated their destination. He didn't want to play games. She'd made it clear where they stood. What the hell had he been thinking to come up here? They'd steal another night, and then what?

"Jess, no. Not like this. I can't do this tonight." Even as the words left his mouth he knew they were bullshit. He'd been dying for her for days. He'd take a stolen night over not ever having her again.

Jessa never hesitated. She pulled him past the bed and into the bathroom. Steam rose from the large bathtub, filling the room with a balmy thickness that fogged the mirror.

"Arms up," she ordered.

Garrett shifted his feet, his muscles already anticipating the water's heat. He lifted his arms and bent forward to make it easier for her to remove his shirt.

"You've been working so hard. I've been selfish these last few days." She dropped his shirt and cupped his face. Her gaze was direct, intense. "I'm sorry, Garrett. It seems I can't stay away from you."

Her delicate lips whispered over his mouth and he fought not to take control. He didn't want to do anything to break the spell she'd woven around him.

"I've missed you. Your smile, your hands ... your tongue." The belt of her robe fell away. "I'm going to make it up to you. Tonight, I'm going to take care of you for a change." She raised a hand to cut off his retort. "No arguments."

Garrett hadn't planned to argue. He was more interested in the naked flesh she revealed as her robe slid from her shoulders. "What do you plan to do?"

A rich, husky laugh escaped her throat. "Bath, massage, food. Maybe a little hanky-panky." She wagged her eyebrows.

Garrett smiled as the dark mood that had plagued him the last few days finally eased off.

"Ahhh, there's my gorgeous man. I wondered where he went."

He tried not to make too much of her referring to him as hers, but the words had his heart pumping overtime.

She bent to remove his shoes and socks. Her hair felt like silk between his fingers. He pinched the clip that held it in place and tossed it aside as the mass of gorgeous waves spilled over her shoulders. Her eyes looked up at him, filled with kindness and compassion.

Holy hell, she was beautiful.

Jessa rose up on her tiptoes and placed a quick kiss on his lips.

"I like the way you look at me."

His stomach rolled as she toyed with his waistband. "How's that?"

She dodged his mouth and pushed his shorts down his legs. "Like you enjoy what you see. Now, in you go," she said, pointing to the tub.

"I definitely enjoy what I see. I'm also kind of enjoying this bossy side of you. Aren't you getting in with me?"

She shoved him forward. "You get in first. Do you need another beer?"

He arched a brow, wondering how she'd known he'd been drinking. "No, I've already had enough. But, thanks." His plan to get drunk was forgotten in lieu of much more pleasurable pursuits.

She nodded and maneuvered him to the tub. He didn't even try to stifle the groan that escaped his throat as the warm water melted into his skin.

"Is it too hot?"

He scanned her naked flesh. "It's perfect."

Jessa tossed a towel on the floor and knelt next to him. She cupped the sides of his head, her fingers massaging his scalp. He moaned with pleasure. "That feels amazing."

"We're just getting started."

As her hands worked their magic, Garrett finally relaxed. His muscles loosened and the weight on his shoulders eased.

Jessa's hands worked down his neck in tender strokes. She caressed his chest, his stomach. When she reached under the water and took his engorged cock in her hand, Garrett sighed. Her slender fingers wrapped around his length and stroked him from root to tip.

Fucking heaven.

She reached down and cupped his balls. "Don't you dare come in the bathwater, Garrett," she admonished. "I still have to wash your hair."

Like hell. She was ten seconds from being pulled into the tub with him. Five, if she kept touching him like that.

"Saucy wench." Garrett grabbed her wrists. "Stop playing with my balls, or we'll have to move to the shower."

Her throaty laugh vibrated down his spine. She palmed a bottle of shampoo and dribbled it over his head. She was good at this; her skilled fingertips were firm against his scalp as she washed the sweat and grime from his hair.

In that moment he knew he'd do anything, go anywhere for this woman. He was putty in her hands.

"Scoot forward and tip your head back. Time to rinse."

Relaxed, his mood vastly improved, Garrett slid forward and dunked himself under the water. A few swipes of his hands over his head and he came up, shampoo free.

Water splashed over the edge as Jessa slid into the tub behind him. Her legs circled and came to rest on his thighs. Garrett arched and wiggled his shoulders to caress her taut nipples with his back.

The gentle rasp of a washcloth brushed over him. He bent forward, giving her more room to work as she moved in slow circles, rubbing in a hypnotizing rhythm. She washed his arms, his chest, his stomach. He soaked up her touch, reveled in the feel of her hands on him.

His cock bobbed in protest at being ignored when her knuckles brushed over the patch of hair at his base and then moved away. She was torturing him and he was powerless against her.

"Feel better?"

"Hmm. I'll say. Almost back to human." He turned so he could look in her eyes. "I'm really sorry I was such an ass."

She should be angry. Rail at him for the way he'd treated her. Instead, she placed a gentle palm against his cheek. The compassion in her eyes killed him. He didn't deserve any of it. Not her or her compassion.

"Do you want to talk about it?"

What was he going to say? That he wanted a relationship with her? That he had no idea how he was ever going to let her go? He wasn't so naive. Things weren't that simple. He wished to God they were.

"No. I want to enjoy this moment."

"It's early yet. There are many more moments to come."

He was counting on it. "And I intend to enjoy them all." A loud knock on the door made Jessa jump. "You expecting someone, princess?"

"I'd better get that."

She started to rise, but he stopped her. He rolled in the water, turned until he faced her, and pulled her onto his lap.

"Garrett?"

He squeezed her in a tight hug. "I missed you too, Jess."

CHAPTER THIRTEEN

Jessa stepped out of the tub, lingering a moment to enjoy the view. Garrett was sex-on-a-stick fully clothed and covered in sweat. Bathtub Garrett was even more tempting. Tanned skin pulled taut over hardened muscles. His strong thighs bunching as he bent his knees and reclined against the back of the tub. His hair teased the tops of his shoulders as drops of water fell from the ends to join the rivulets running down his chest. Wet strands fell around to grace his cheekbones and Jessa reached out to smooth them back. He was spectacular.

And he'd missed her.

The knock sounded again.

"That's dinner. Guess I lost track of the time." She pulled a large terrycloth robe off the hook behind the door and wrapped herself in it. "Stay and enjoy your bath. I'll be back in a bit."

She leaned over and kissed his forehead, trailing her fingers through his mess of hair. If she didn't get out of here, they'd miss dinner for sure. "Don't do anything you shouldn't," she called out as she pulled the bathroom door closed behind her.

"One second," she yelled as she pulled on a pair of shorts and the T-shirt she'd gotten from Garrett the other night. She loved the feel of the soft cotton against her skin. She'd slept in it every night, his lingering scent reminding her of what they'd shared.

God, she'd missed being with him.

The last few days had been agony.

Her body came alive when Garrett was within sight, as if it recalled how well his hands molded to its every curve. Her muscles went soft, moist heat formed between her legs every time he glanced her way.

And still she'd remained at arm's length. Fighting like hell to remember her purpose here wasn't to sleep with Garrett, but to make friends with him, guide him through the rough spots and keep him out of trouble.

Something told her she wouldn't be getting a raise any time soon.

The concierge rolled a cart through, pausing inside the door. "Is there any place in particular you'd like me to set up, miss?"

Jessa laughed. He couldn't be more than a year or two younger than her. At least he hadn't called her ma'am. She motioned for him to follow her. "Here is fine," she said, waving her hand toward the table.

"How many guests are you expecting?"

The staff at this hotel could be trusted, but Jessa didn't want to broadcast that Garrett was here.

Or that he's currently naked in the bathtub. "Excuse me?"

"I apologize, would you prefer I place all the plates for you to sort out for seating?"

Jessa was still confused. "I'm not expecting company."

He nodded in understanding, a slight smile on his face. He opened the cart and Jessa felt her face flush.

"Wow, that does look like a lot of food, doesn't it?"

"If you don't mind me saying, miss, I hope you're hungry."

Jessa had called the hotel's chef and personally requested that a special menu be prepared. She'd never actually believed he could pull it off on such short notice. Yet she watched, amazed, as the concierge presented her with all the greatest Southern comfort foods, or so he claimed as he pulled plate after plate and set them on the table.

If a bath and massage didn't improve Garrett's mood, maybe good ole Southern cooking would do the trick.

"Thank you for doing this on such short notice." Jessa knew the concierge didn't have anything to do with the meal preparation, but after he'd finished, she slipped him a twenty anyway.

"You're quite welcome, miss. It's our pleasure to serve you.

Oh, and here is the item you requested." He handed her a plastic bag bearing the hotel logo. Nodding once, he smiled. "Enjoy your evening."

"What's in the bag?" Garrett asked as the concierge slipped from the room.

"You're supposed to be in the bath." Jessa reached in and pulled out a plastic bottle filled with a rich yellow liquid. "I called the spa downstairs and asked them to send up whatever they had to use on sore muscles." She held the bottle up for his inspection. "This is supposed to be a mixture of jojoba and essential oils. I have it on good authority that it will work out all of your kinks."

"Hmm. You wanna work out my kinks?" He wagged his brows. "'Cause that could be downright interesting."

His hooded gaze caught her breath. Damn, the man was sexy. "Do you want to eat first?"

Her stomach filled with overactive butterflies. Now that Garrett was here, the food seemed like a ridiculous idea. What did she know about making him happy? She didn't know anything about him. Not really. She knew who he was as a baseball player, knew every statistic about his career practically since Little League. She knew his smile could melt her insides and his gaze could make her wet.

She knew how he fucked.

But that didn't tell her anything about who he was as a man. His hopes, his dreams.

She could please him with her body, satisfy him sexually. But out of the bedroom? No clue.

"Depends on what's on the menu." He looked her up and down. "Nice shirt."

Jessa's body warmed, her clit pulsating in anticipation of the promise in his voice. She cleared her throat. "I had the chef prepare things I thought might help you feel better. Although chicken fried steak with mashed potatoes, paired with all that gravy will definitely call for an extra workout."

Surprise widened his eyes. "You had that made for me?"

She nodded, darting her gaze away to hide her embarrassment.

Inspecting under the lids, Garrett's eyes drifted closed as he inhaled the delicious scents. "Damn. I don't know what to say."

He turned and scooped her up, one arm cradling her legs, the other pressed against her back, as he urged her mouth to his. He pressed his tongue against her lips and she opened, sucking him in, loving the feel of being in his arms.

"Thank you, sweetheart. But don't drop that bottle," he said between kisses. "We're about to put it to good use."

The endearment wrapped around her heart. It was different somehow, from calling her princess. More intimate. Erotic images of Garrett naked and slathered in oil had her squirming, desperate to get her hands all over his warm, tanned skin. As well as the skin that wasn't so tanned.

By the time they reached the bedroom, dinner forgotten, Jessa was ready to throw him to the mattress and ride them both to ecstasy.

Garrett placed her on her feet and stripped off his robe, his magnificent body exposed for her pleasure.

"Lay down." Her voice trembled in time with the flutter in her pussy.

"That's not really what I had in mind, princess." He shoved a hand under her shirt and cupped her breast, teasing the tip with his thumb.

"Uh-uh. You first."

"That's what I'm counting on." He pinched her nipple and tugged.

The sensation shot through her breast, tightening her stomach. The twinge of pain ramping her arousal until her pussy wept with need. Wiggling out of his grasp, she spun him and pointed. "No, *you* first. On the bed. Now. So I can work on your muscles."

"Oh, I've got a muscle you can work," he teased.

"Garrett!" She popped him on his bare ass and shoved him forward.

Laughing, he stretched out on the bed, his naked backside making her mouth water. He folded his arms and rested his cheek against his folded hands.

Having Garrett at her disposal was too delicious an opportunity to pass up. He'd learned every inch of her body. He'd tasted her, teased her, threatened to do things to her that made her body heat to an uncomfortable level.

He'd shown her how to appreciate herself as a woman. In his arms, she could be anything, say anything, do anything.

It was addictive. And it was her turn.

The last few nights she'd lain awake, her body painfully aware of Garrett's absence. It was insane, but just once, she wanted to wake up wrapped in his arms. If he happened to wake her in the middle of the night because he couldn't wait another minute to take her, well, that would be okay too.

She eased over him, straddling his ass. His heat penetrated her skin and she resisted rubbing on him like a cat, instead pouring a small amount of oil into her hands and rubbing them together.

Starting at the base of his spine, she leaned in, using her body weight to add subtle pressure. Her hands warmed, a combination of the oil and the heat from their combined body temperatures.

Long, wide strokes spread the oil. She massaged her thumbs up either side of his spine, trailing across his shoulders and looping around once again, hugging his ribcage and trim waistline before returning to where she'd started. The man had an amazing body. Jessa could get lost tracing all its sleek lines and hard edges. She especially liked the way his muscles tapered the lower she went, ending in two of the most delicious dimples above his ass.

She ran her fingers across the line between pale and sun-kissed skin, thinking very soon she'd trace that line with her tongue.

Maybe next time she'd request flavored oil.

Using the heels of her palms in slow, circular strokes, Jessa worked her way up his back, eliciting moans of pleasure from Garrett. His muscles were hard, strong. Tight. She moved to work between his shoulder blades, pressing in with her thumbs, sweeping out and circling back to lengthen and relax.

"Jesus, your hands are magical," Garrett growled.

Jessa moved to his upper shoulders, her breasts grazing his back as she hooked her hands around him, uncaring if she got oil on her shirt. She drew in a breath and her nipples reacted, shrinking into tender buds.

"How does the oil feel?" Jessa continued to work across his broad shoulders, then switched to the pads of her fingers to work up the back of his neck.

He adjusted his head to give her better access. "It's weird. It feels hot and cold all at the same time. Strangely soothing." He sighed. "But then again, with your hands on me, baby, there's no way it could be anything but."

"What a sweet talker you are, Garrett Donovan. One day, that silver tongue of yours is gonna get you in trouble."

His husky chuckle rumbled through her legs and traveled to her core. "Tonight, if I'm lucky."

"Like I said." She moved back down his spine, shifting her body until she straddled his legs. Tiny hairs tickled her skin as she cupped the cheeks of his ass. Firm, like the rest of him.

She dug her fingers into his flesh, kneading the fine globes until he grew restless. She swatted him and jolted as his head whipped around.

"What do you think you're doing, princess?"

She soothed the skin with the palm of her hand. "Couldn't resist." Distracted, she watched as blood reached the surface and turned his ass cheek light pink.

"That's twice you've popped my ass. I think a little retribution is in order."

The pulse of her heart pounded heavy in her ears. His words worried and excited her at the same time. She wasn't worried he'd hurt her. Never that. She worried what it said about her that she was so ready to play this little game. What would he think when he found her swollen and wet? Would he think less of her?

No. Of course he wouldn't. He'd encouraged her, praised the way she'd made him feel. This could be an opportunity to push her limits, and maybe his, too.

She'd started it and she wasn't about to chicken out now.

She eased her leg over, sliding off the bed. "What kind of retribution?"

His gaze followed her, eyes flashing with a hunger she felt clear to her toes.

"The kind that puts my palm on your bare ass. Among other places." He rolled over and pushed from the bed, standing his full height. He twisted left, then right, testing the muscles she'd worked. His cock, swollen and thick, hung heavy between his legs. Moisture beaded at its tip and Jessa fought the urge to drop to her knees and take him in her mouth.

"Because you've been so generous tonight," he fisted his length and stroked once, twice. "I'll give you a three-second head start."

Jessa couldn't pull her gaze away from his hand. The dominance in the way he spoke, the confidence in the way he gripped himself, shifted something inside her. The knowledge that she wanted this, wanted Garrett more than she'd ever thought possible, heightened the anticipation. She licked her lips and inhaled slowly. Her heart hammered in her chest.

"One."

Oh, shit.

Did he really expect her to run? The wicked gleam in his eyes told her yes. He expected her to run, and was prepared to give chase.

"Two."

Jessa backed away as he made to circle around her. He moved slowly, stalking her. The door at her back, she knew this was her only chance.

"Three."

* * *

Garrett couldn't even muster a laugh when Jessa squealed and dashed from the room. He needed every bit of lung power just to breathe.

Fucking unhinged. That's what she did to him.

This little game they'd started had his dick close to bursting. It'd been hard enough to let her play on his skin, her hands kneading away his aches and pains, her fingers dancing over every inch of his back, his sides, his ass.

He clamped down on the base of his shaft and took a steadying breath. Wouldn't do any good to lose it now. He had plans for his little princess tonight. He'd make her wait a bit longer, drag out the anticipation while he cooled off.

In the bathroom, Garrett grabbed his shorts and wrestled his wallet from the pocket. He tossed it, along with his key card and change, onto the counter. He wouldn't need those things tonight. If he had his way, he wouldn't need that goddamn key card for the next forty-eight hours.

Unless he went for a change of clothes.

He wasn't leaving Jessa tonight. Hell, he wasn't leaving Jessa, period. The idea settled over him like a warm blanket.

Not sure when it happened, the mind shift about Jessa. When she'd told him his touch was the one she desired ... the moment he sank into her precious heat that first time ... maybe the minute he'd answered his phone tonight.

He didn't give a fuck about the when's or why's. How he'd gotten here didn't really matter, did it?

Jessa was his. Would be his. He didn't know how yet, but he knew they'd make it work.

It wasn't like her dad could kill him or anything.

No, he'd just fire his ass and leave him with nothing but a farm and a family to support.

Fuck that. Garrett would find a way for them to be together. Even if that meant going toe-to-toe with her father. TJ liked him, and the feeling was mutual. He could work with that.

All he had to do now was convince Jessa.

With that in mind, he finished collecting their clothes from the wet floor and tossed them into a chair in the bedroom.

Now where was that ... ah, yes.

His gaze landed on what he needed. This time he did chuckle. How far would she let him go? How far did he want to go?

Questions he'd never been compelled to explore until her.

So far, their relationship had been about sex. And baseball. Two of his favorite things, yes. But he wanted them to be about more than that, something far more intimate. He wanted her in his life, in his house, in his bed.

He wanted it all.

"Garrett?" Jessa's voice drifted from the other room, quiet, shaky. Excited.

Beginning right now.

CHAPTER FOURTEEN

The wait was killing her. What was taking him so long?

Jessa's heart thumped. She moved around the couch — a poor barrier against an aroused, determined male — apprehension coiling in her stomach.

"Garrett?" She kept her voice soft, expecting him to jump out at her at any moment.

"Did you think I'd let you get away, princess?" Garrett's tone, deep and rich, rolled over her as he sauntered into the room.

Her clit was quick to answer, throbbing in response. "What is that?"

He raised his hand.

Oh, God.

The belt from a hotel robe hung from his fist. "After spanking my ass and running away, I figured I'd need some help keeping you where I wanted." He tilted his head to the side, considering her. "You seemed to enjoy spanking my ass, Jessa. I wonder if I'll enjoy spanking yours."

Jessa pressed the heel of her palm into her stomach and bit her lip to keep from coming on the spot. "You told me to run."

He shook his head. "I gave you the option of a head start if you *wanted* to run. The decision was yours, baby." Garrett approached her with slow, deliberate steps. "Are you going to run again?"

Run? She couldn't even breathe. How the hell was she supposed to run? She shook her head.

One side of his mouth curled up as his gaze darkened. "Give me your hands."

She hesitated long enough that he took a step back.

"Are you scared?" He studied her. "Because we don't have —"

"No," she whispered. The idea of being tied and at his disposal was her undoing. Liquid rushed from between her legs and she squeezed her knees together, embarrassed he'd notice how much she wanted this, him. Jessa thrust her hands out. "Not scared."

Not verbal either, apparently. She prayed he didn't need further words, because she didn't think she had any. Already, her body was prepared for him. More than prepared. It was waving the white flag of surrender.

Fitting analogy since he's about to bind her.

Garrett stared at her as if trying to read her thoughts. Seemingly satisfied with what he saw, he nodded once and reached out, stripping the shirt over her head and letting it fall to the floor.

"Perfect," he said, smiling his approval at her bare breasts. He turned her, bringing her wrists together at the base of her back and securing them with the belt. His fingers lingered, tracing up her arms, leaving tiny goose bumps in their wake. "God, your skin is so soft." His mouth was against her ear. "And such a pretty blush. That better not be a self-conscious blush, Jessa."

Already he knew her so well.

"If you could see how fucking gorgeous you are right now ..." He nipped at her earlobe, teasing the ridge with his tongue. "Just you and me, Jessa. No shame. Only pleasure."

No shame. She didn't have the energy for shame when all she could think about was what he'd do next. The excitement of the unexpected, the thrill of sharing this experience with Garrett, left her light-headed.

He cupped her breasts, raising them, squeezing them together as his thumbs teased the sensitive peaks.

Jessa groaned as her head fell back against his chest. Arousal pumped through her veins, driving her crazy with need.

He settled a hand against her stomach, comforting and warm, as he pulled her tight against him. The hard ridge of his cock pressed against her. Wanting to touch him, she wiggled her fingers through the coarse hair at his base. It was all she could manage with her bound wrists.

"Oh, no you don't." He shifted, keeping himself out of her reach. He teased the waistband of her shorts and she drew her stomach drew in, giving him room to slip inside. "Have you ever done anything like this before?"

Again, she shook her head. Her eyes drifted closed as he caressed her mound, avoiding where she needed him the most. Not only had she never done anything like this before, but Garrett was the only man who'd ever gotten her this worked up.

The rough pads of his fingertips stoked the fire that seemed to linger whenever he was close. He brushed the top of her slit, teasing, taunting her. Frustrated, she rolled her hips, trying to entice him lower.

His voice held a slight tremble, from excitement or nervousness, she didn't know, didn't care.

She needed him to touch her.

"Me neither. But something tells me I'm going to enjoy the hell out of this." He pulled his hand from her shorts.

Damn it.

"There." He raised his chin. "Bend over the end of the couch, Jessa. Legs apart."

"Garrett." His name escaped her lips with a puff of breath.

His hand slid back down her belly, back under the waistband of her shorts. He cupped her pussy, trailing a finger over the swollen lips. A sound, pure male and guttural, came from his throat. "My God, you're so wet." In one swift movement, he yanked her shorts down her legs. "Step out."

Obeying as quickly as possible, she kicked her shorts away. Garrett turned her, pulling her close and crushing his lips to hers. Licking. Biting. Tasting. He kissed her like he owned her, cherished her.

Without her hands, Jessa had to rely on her lips, her tongue to show him what he did to her. She met him, thrust for thrust. His flavor infusing her mouth until she knew she'd never be free of it.

He broke away, chest heaving. Jessa allowed herself a small smile of satisfaction. At least she wasn't the only one in pain here. The hot, insistent, length of him pressed into her stomach and she knew he wanted this as much as she did. She squirmed a little, delighting in the feel of his rough palms as they drifted up the back of her thighs, teased the crease of her ass and caressed over her cheeks.

His hand landed without warning, sharp and fast.

Jessa jumped and cried out, the sound of his hand on her bare ass reverberating in her ears.

"Shhh," Garrett soothed, his lips a whisper across her forehead. He landed another smack on the opposite side before smoothing his palms over her again. "Wait for it."

Sting, followed by a delicious warmth. Pleasant. Arousing.

Unexpected.

"The couch. Now," he demanded.

On unsteady feet, Jessa moved, Garrett's heat at her back as he moved with her.

It was tricky, trying to bend over the furniture without the use of her hands. A face plant would really kill the mood right now. But Garrett didn't let her get that far.

He latched onto the binding at her wrists, settling her hands in the bend of her back. His hold was firm, reassuring, as tapped the inside of her foot with his.

"Spread your legs. Wider. That's it."

A shiver racked her body as his palm pressed between her shoulder blades, trailing a path down her spine as she lowered herself into position.

Exposed.

That was the only word that came to mind.

Naked, legs spread and open, her body was his to do with as he pleased.

Awareness of her situation burned into her chest. Here she was, naked and bound, with a man she'd only known a short time. Yet there was no panic, no fear. Only trust. Trust that Garrett would take care of her, freeing her from the bonds of worry and allowing her to just *feel*.

It was liberating.

A popping sound got her attention. She craned her neck to watch through the corner of her eye as Garrett slicked his hands with their massage oil.

"What are you doing?" She didn't want a massage, she wanted him inside her. Now would be good.

Please, now.

His grin was wicked, devious. "Had an idea."

Jessa sucked in a breath as he reached around and tweaked her nipples, coating them with oil before moving away again.

She whimpered, the buds pulling impossibly tighter, her breasts growing heavy with desire. "Are you trying to kill me?"

Smoothing a hand over her ass, Garrett paused to squeeze her cheeks before traveling down between her legs. Jessa's knees buckled as his fingers spread her open, then swiped over her sensitive bud.

Heat blasted through her. Followed by an intense chill. Hot, cold. Back and forth until her head spun. Her nipples, her ass cheeks, her pussy. Everywhere Garrett touched with his oiled hands was a maelstrom of sensation and convulsing flesh. Her pussy was aching with emptiness, weeping to be filled. Needing more.

And more was what he gave her.

Sparks traveled through her as his hand cracked against her ass again. Once, twice. Alternating one side for the other.

"You're fucking beautiful, Jessa," he panted behind her. "Your ass pink and warm from my hand. Are you okay, baby? That oil doing what I expected?"

Brutal honesty was all she had now, his play flaying her alive. "Goddamn it, Garrett. Fuck me. I'll go crazy if you don't fuck me, I swear it."

"I'll take that as a yes." He slid two fingers inside her and her body rejoiced, clamping down hard to keep him there.

So close, she was so damn close.

"You like that, don't you, Jessa? Jesus, you're dripping. So fucking hot. Do you want more, baby?"

"Yes," she cried out as he teased her inner walls. "Please." She moved her hips, riding his fingers like she wanted to ride his cock. Tears burned her eyes as pleasure engulfed her, surged through her veins.

A tormented cry escaped her lips as he pulled his fingers out of her.

And then, blessed heavens, the broad head of his cock pushed at her entrance, her arousal and the oil providing him slick passage.

"Oh, God, yes …" She opened around him, stretched taut, nerve endings firing on all cylinders.

"Jesus. Fuck," he growled.

"Don't stop, Garrett. Don't …" She pushed back into him, fighting to take him deeper, her muscles shaking with the effort to hold herself up.

"Holy shit."

Jessa peered over her shoulder. Garrett was fixated on where they were joined, his eyes wide, dark with unspent lust, his jaw clenched tight.

"What's wrong?"

"Fuck," he said again, shuddering as his gaze met hers. "I must have gotten oil on my … fuck." The syllable dragged out as his eyes rolled and drifted closed, his head falling back on his shoulders.

"God, that feels ... you feel incredible. So hot, so tight." Cursing, he grabbed her binding and jerked her back. "Since you can't hold on, I'll do it for you, because I'm about to fuck the shit out of you."

"About damn time." She squeezed her inner muscles, fighting to keep him inside as he eased away.

"Remember you said that," he warned. Slamming back into her, he set a heady pace.

Time and space no longer had meaning. Only masculine grunts, feminine mewls. Garrett drilling inside her, filling her, surrounding her. The sweet scent of sweat, the sounds of slick sex filled the room as, together, they chased the sun.

Her skin, damp with perspiration, tingled with the telltale sign of impending orgasm. Her spine curled, raising her ass higher. She moaned as Garrett filled her, deep to her sensitive core.

"Come, Jessa. I want to feel you explode around me." Garrett's firm demand, coupled with his furious pace, sent her over the edge.

Stars exploded behind her eyes, bells rang her ears. Her muscles drew tight as her body released in a rush. The room spun as wave after wave crashed through her, leaving her shattered with its intensity.

Behind her, Garrett shouted his release, his hips continuing to pump until they were both spent.

Jessa's head sagged forward, her breath sawing in and out. "Never ... done that ... before, huh?"

Her hands were released. Weak, exhausted, Jessa dropped forward, letting her cheek rest against the couch cushions, her arms spread out above her head.

"Nope." He fell over her, his weight crushing what little air she'd managed to get back in her lungs.

"Home run," she sighed.

He snorted. "You're going to be the death of me."

"Good, then we're even."

A chill met her back as he raised up, easing her upright and turning her to face him. His palm touched her cheek in a sweet caress. "I didn't hurt you, did I? I mean, I know I —"

"Garrett, stop." She placed a finger to his lips. "You didn't hurt me." The sting of his hand had been replaced with a much nicer sensation. Tingling warmth that told her she'd be sore tomorrow. She grinned at him. "At least, not in a bad way."

"Come on, princess. Let's get you cleaned up so we can eat."

He took her hand and led her toward the bathroom.

"Worked up an appetite, have you?" she teased.

He grinned over his shoulder. "I hope you ordered a lot of food, because I've only begun to work on my appetite, baby."

She raised a brow and glanced down, admiring his fantastic ass. "Are you planning to stay awhile?"

"I plan to stay longer than that, princess. I'm off tomorrow, so there's no need to rush." He released her long enough to start the shower, then pulled her inside with him.

As if they'd never touched before, they washed each other with slow precision. Learning every line and crease, memorizing every sound with every caress.

"So." Jessa circled his nipple with her fingertip, delighting in his husky growl. "What are you going to do tomorrow?"

Garrett took her hand and brought it to his mouth, kissing each finger before placing a final kiss to her palm. "Anything that includes you. Maybe we can get out, have some fun?"

"What've you got in mind?"

"Leave it to me. You trust me, right?" He kissed the tip of her nose.

She laughed. "I think that goes without saying at this point." She hesitated, wanting to ask him to stay, but not sure how. She wanted to know what it felt like to have him next to her, to wake up in his arms.

"Garrett, um ..."

He lifted her chin and placed a soft kiss on her lips. "What is it, princess?"

"You're, well ... you're staying here tonight, right? I mean ... will you stay with me?"

His features softened as his hand slid around to cup her neck. He lifted her to him, pressing his mouth to hers in a fiery kiss that left them both panting. "I wouldn't have it any other way."

Jessa was filled with emotion. He'd give her tonight, and she'd keep the memory tucked deep, knowing it would be little comfort when this was over.

She wrapped her arms around his neck, afraid to let go, afraid to hang on.

Garrett Donovan had stolen her heart.

CHAPTER FIFTEEN

"No, Garrett."

"Come on, Jessa."

"You seriously want me to ride that? I'll get all wet!"

His lids fell shut and he cursed under his breath. "I promise it won't hurt, and it'll be over before you know it. You might even enjoy it."

Jessa looked up at the ginormous water ride and her stomach turned itself inside out. Nervousness paralyzed her limbs. She shook her head. "I can't feel my legs."

"I'll be with you the whole time," he promised.

She swallowed a gulp and shook her head again. No way was she getting on that thing. Not in this lifetime.

"It's perfectly safe," he purred at her.

She poked him in the chest. "No fair using your sexy voice on me."

"I have a sexy voice?" He blinked his beautiful eyes and gave her a look that was more rogue than innocent.

"Yes, damn it, you do. Stop using it."

He leaned in. "You shouldn't have told me that. I'll use any tactic to get my way."

"You wouldn't."

His lips quirked as he crossed his arms over his chest. "I would."

"I'm the 'keep my feet on the ground' kind of girl. Not the 'ride a log up fifty stories and then plummet to the earth' kind of girl."

He threw his head back and laughed. "You're exaggerating, Jess. It's not fifty stories."

"But the sign said —"

"Fifty feet, princess. Feet. Not stories."

"Oh," she said, sarcasm dripping from her voice. "That makes it all better then."

She didn't know how long they'd waited, but it wasn't near enough time to get her nerves in check. When Garrett had mentioned spending the day together, she'd imagined he'd want to stay in, stay naked. Order a pizza. Maybe catch a game on the TV. But this … this she hadn't expected.

"Come on, we didn't stand in line all this time so you could back out." He laughed and grabbed her hand, pulling her with him as the hallowed out log that would carry them to their deaths arrived. He gave her a sexy smile. "This is nothing. Be glad I'm not taking you on the roller coasters."

"What are you? Some kind of adrenaline junkie?"

He ignored her. "In you go."

She glared at him as he helped her into her seat at the front. "You so owe me for this."

He gave her cheek a quick peck, then hopped into the seat behind her. "Looking forward to paying up, sweetheart."

Jessa closed her eyes and prayed she could get through this without throwing up. Nervous energy flowed and she felt her cheeks grow warm with … what? Fear? Anticipation?

The ride jerked to a start and they were on their way. A warm, heavy weight squeezed her shoulder in reassurance and she craned her neck, catching the heat that flashed in his eyes as his thumb caressed the back of her neck, just for a second, before pulling away again.

Within minutes, she'd forgotten her fears and was lost in the magic of the ride. She giggled at the banjo-playing animatronic rabbit, the hillbilly music, the happy squeals of the children behind her. By the time the warning signs signified danger ahead, when they started to climb the steep slope, she was enchanted.

As they neared the top, awareness had her knuckles whitening on the bar over her lap and she squeezed her eyes shut, holding her breath.

"Breathe, Jess. And open your eyes!"

At the demand in Garrett's voice, Jessa's eyes snapped open as they hovered for a split second before plummeting down the other side. She screamed as the ground raced to meet them. Water splashed over her, its chill shocking, refreshing.

She laughed with genuine glee, her heart racing in her chest as the ride came to an end.

Garrett was there to help her out and she threw herself at him, her breasts crushed into his chest as she hugged his neck. "That ... that was ... exhilarating!" He spun her around and tiny droplets of water flew from the ends of her hair. She didn't even care that she was wet. Her body shook as adrenaline pumped through her. She felt amazing.

Alive.

The same way she felt whenever Garrett touched her.

Her feet touched the ground as he released her. He backed away and scowled.

"What's the matter?"

His eyes were glued to her chest. She looked down, gasped and plucked at the thin, pink shirt that clung to her breasts. Her bra did nothing to hide her nipples, currently poking through the material.

"Shit!" She looked around to see if anyone else noticed her predicament. There were several others around her who were soaked, but she had drawn several male stares.

She crossed her arms over her chest and looked at Garrett when a thought occurred. "Why aren't you wet?"

A guilty grin split his face. "I ducked."

"Oh! You!" She moved for him again, but he grabbed her wrists and held them tight against his chest.

"We have bigger problems right now, princess. Add it to my list of things you get to pay me back for." He laced their hands and merged them into the flow of foot traffic.

"Where are we going?" She stumbled, trying to keep up as he pulled her along.

"We're going to buy you a new shirt."

"I'll admit that's probably a good idea, but do you have to pull my shoulder out of its socket in the process?" She jerked on his hand to make her point.

He turned on her, eyes blazing. "I'm not real fond of sharing what's mine, Jessa. And right now, anyone who looks can see your ..." He clamped his mouth shut and resumed their march.

"Garrett, I ... do you ... you think I'm yours?" The thought made her ridiculously happy.

"For today, yes. Make no mistake about it. I don't have any plans to share what little time I have left with you, and I certainly won't allow other men to see the delicious secrets you hide under your clothes."

He stopped in front of a store.

"You're cute when you're jealous." She bit back a laugh at his deep scowl. Still reeling from his possessiveness, Jessa fought against the idea that they would soon be going their separate ways. She wanted to hang on to this feeling for a little longer, a feeling that could very well destroy her in the end.

He slapped some cash in her hand. "Get a new shirt." He glanced at her chest and grimaced. "Preferably one darker than the color of your bra."

She looked at the cash and passed it back him, snickering. "I don't need your money, Garrett."

When he didn't take it, she pressed it in his palm. "I can buy my own shirt." She turned to enter the store. "But, you can buy me something sweet for going on that ride with you to begin with," she said over her shoulder.

Jessa didn't waste any time in the store. She picked out a black shirt and giggled at the word *princess* emblazoned across the front. Perfect. She asked the cashier to cut the tag off so she could wear it out.

Garrett squinted at her before his lips curled up. "Wow. That's sexy." He took her hand and spun her in a circle.

She fluffed her soaked hair, thankful she hadn't worn much makeup. 'Cause that would have been a disaster. "Yeah, right. I look like a drowned rat. I had to put this on over my wet shirt, so it's still not helping with much more than covering me."

"That's good enough for me. Now, you asked for something sweet." He craned his neck to see over the crowd of people. "Let's go."

Again, he laced their fingers, tugging her to follow him. She shouldn't let him hold her hand. And she shouldn't have let her excitement get the best of her when she hugged him after their ride. They were in public for chrissake.

Not very stealthy of them, but Jessa enjoyed the feel of his strong fingers wrapped around hers, the feel of his calloused thumb brushing across the inside of her wrist. Enjoyed it too much to pull away.

No one stared or pointed, no one gawked or commented. Today, they were two people amongst thousands of other people too caught up in their own enjoyment to notice something as insignificant as Garrett holding her hand. How could something simple enough to be ignored hold such meaning for her?

Garrett took her into a bakery and proceeded to order two of the biggest cinnamon rolls Jessa had ever seen, along with two bottles of water.

Once they were seated, she eyed the confection. "If I eat all this, I'll go into diabetic shock."

Frowning, Garrett reached for her plate. "You don't eat sweets?"

She palmed her fork, wielding it like a dagger. "It was a joke. Back off my pastry, dude."

Garrett showed her his palms and eased away as she dug in, shoving an oversized bite into her mouth. She hummed around the sticky goo, trying not to laugh and spew crumbs across the table. Her eyes rolled back in her head in ecstasy as the delicious flavor melted over her tongue. She was pretty sure she had icing on her face.

Smirking, Garrett watched her. "I think that's about the sexiest thing I've ever seen."

Jessa cupped her hand to her mouth, losing her battle not to laugh. She worked her throat, choking down what she could before reaching for her bottle of water to wash down the rest.

She wiped her mouth on a napkin. "Yeah, well, if you keep looking at me like that, I'll never be able to eat in front of you again."

He leaned in. "I don't know which I'd rather eat. You or the cinnamon roll."

"Why not both?" she said, watching him track her tongue as she licked over her lips.

Garrett shifted in his seat. "I'm not in the mood to get arrested for fucking you on this table, as tempting as the thought may be." He used the edge of his fork to slice through the roll on his plate. His eyes met hers again as he brought it to her lips. "Open up, baby."

Mesmerized by the erotic tone of his voice, Jessa opened and let him feed her. She closed her lips over the fork as he eased it from her mouth. His gaze dropped to her throat as she swallowed.

"Delicious."

"I couldn't agree more."

"Your turn," she said as she cut a piece and offered it to him.

Back and forth they went, alternating feeding each other, oblivious to the world around them. Jessa forgot all the reasons they shouldn't be together for the one reason they should.

She loved him. And not that sweet, flowery crush shit that people their age seemed to have. Hers was a deep, intense yearning. A desire that threatened to burn her alive. A need to possess and be possessed.

"I'd give anything to know what you are thinking about right now." Hunger burned in Garrett's eyes as she dragged a finger through the leftover icing on her plate.

Jessa brought her finger to her mouth, rubbing the icing across her lips before licking it off. She focused all her emotion — her love and her need — into one look. "Are you ready to go back to the hotel?"

His nostrils flared as his chest expanded. "I'll race you to the car."

* * *

It had been an amazing day. In fact, Garrett couldn't remember ever enjoying a day more. He hadn't wanted it to end.

He ran his fingers through Jessa's hair, reveling in the delicious mews she made each time he caressed the silky tresses. She moved her head, snuggling deeper into his lap. If she kept this up, she'd find her resting place a little less comfortable.

No matter how many times he had her, it was never enough. He stayed hard whenever she was around. Hell, fact was, all he had to do was *think* about her. Her smile, her laugh. The way her lips stretched around him as he sank to the back of her throat, the way she'd cupped her breasts and rode him to insanity.

The way she looked at him when she was about to come.

He groaned as blood rushed his groin. She made a noise in protest as his length pressed hard against her cheek. He could take her again — right here, right now — and he knew she wouldn't deny him. His dick may be on board with the idea, but he enjoyed watching her sleep. The rhythmic pace of her breath. Her quiet little sighs. She looked almost angelic. Quite different from the woman who'd begged him to take her harder a few hours ago.

He continued to stroke her hair, his gaze turning back to the basketball game on the TV, while his attention remained on the beauty in his lap.

Their time was coming to an end. Her suitcases were out. Strewn across the room, ready to be packed, and with them, whisk her out of his life. They both felt it. The frantic way they'd fucked all afternoon proved it. It was as if they were trying to cram a lifetime of memories, of pleasure, into one day. And it irritated the shit out of him.

They should have more time. Hell, they should have all the time in the world.

There had to be a way. After all, her dad liked him. Hand selected him out of hundreds of other guys. Garrett was a good man. He wasn't without fault, but he took care of his own. He was loyal and hard working. He didn't play games unless it was on the ball field. He wasn't interested in the bed hopping so many of the other rookies took part in. TJ should have no objections to Garrett dating his daughter.

And he was rationalizing to make himself feel better.

He wanted time, damn it. Time to learn all the little things. The big things. And everything in between.

Time to figure out the emotion pooling in the center of his chest.

Garrett didn't like feeling as if he didn't have a choice. Others dictated so much of his life, he'd be damned if he'd let anyone dictate his love life as well. And yet ...

"Hmm." Jessa shifted, drawing his gaze. He smoothed a hand over her head, her hair soft against his roughened hands.

She made him lose his damn mind like no other woman before her. Drove him crazy with need. And not only the need to lose himself in the sweet heaven of her body, but with the need to wrap his arms around her and keep her safe.

They needed to talk. He couldn't let her go back to New York without knowing how he felt. Even if he hadn't worked it out for himself yet, it was obvious there was something between them. Something more than a couple weeks of stolen moments.

When he was with Jessa, he didn't have to wonder at her motives. When she looked at him, she didn't see a number or a name. Lord knows she didn't need either. He could relax and be himself.

He'd never been in love before, but he wasn't so stubborn as to deny the possibility.

"Garrett?" Her soft, sleep-laden voice soothed him.

Tomorrow. He had to go back to work, but he'd take her to dinner and they'd talk. Because he wasn't letting her go.

"Are you ready to go to bed, sweetheart?" He used the remote to dim the lights before turning off the TV.

She sat up, rubbing her eyes. She reached her arms wide, arching her back in a stretch. "Sorry I fell asleep on you." She smothered a yawn and chuckled. "Guess you wore me out."

He stood and reached for her hand. "Come on, sleepyhead. It's back to reality tomorrow, so we better get some shut eye."

She groaned and dragged her feet behind him. "Can't we stay holed up in this room forever?"

She had no idea how close he was to doing that very thing. He stared as she peeled the clothes from her body and crawled into bed. His gaze lingered long enough to see the flush of arousal color her skin. God, he'd never get enough of this woman.

He pulled his own clothes off and got into bed, pulling her back against his chest. His hand slid over her hip and down the top of her thigh.

"I want you." Her whispered words wrapped around him as she arched her back, her ass grinding against his swollen cock.

Desire rocked his system as he moved her leg back, draping it over his, opening her to him. He guided his length until the sweet heat of her pussy kissed his tip. His hand on her hip to steady them, he eased forward, gritting his teeth against the pleasure that engulfed him.

He moved in a slow, steady rhythm, working himself into her. He wouldn't rush. He wanted to savor the feel of her surrounding him, swallowing him inch by inch.

Inch. By. Fucking. Inch.

"You feel so good," she whispered. "So good."

"Never better, baby." Garrett nipped at the curve of her ear as he reached to cup her breast. He rolled her nipple with his fingers, teasing, tugging, flicking until she groaned his name.

"Tell me what you need, Jess. Tell me what you want." He kept his pace slow, easing in and out, as she fought to drive him faster.

She pushed his hand away from her breast, replacing it with her own. Her pussy clamped down on him when she grabbed her own nipple and squeezed. "Touch me. Rub my clit. Make me come, Garrett. Make us both come. I want to feel you burn inside me."

His control snapped. Garrett pushed her flat to the bed and braced his hands beside her head. He pulled back, using his knees to spread her legs, and buried himself to the hilt within her. He eased back again, only to slam forward once more, his hips smacking against her ass.

His soft, sweet Jessa didn't like easy. She wanted to be taken. Stripped of all thought and decision, she wanted a man who would command her pleasure as well as his own.

And he was that man.

He shifted to his elbows. Reaching under her, Garrett slipped a finger through her wet sex. He moved further, slipping inside her, curling his finger alongside his dick, causing them both to groan at the sensation.

He slid back to her clit, pinching and rolling the hard nub between his fingers. Her pussy rippled around him and he knew she was close.

"Yes, oh God," she choked out.

"That's it. Feel how it is between us. How hot, how sweet. God, I could fuck you forever, Jessa." Garrett pounded into her now, shifting them until Jessa braced her hands against the headboard to stop them from smashing into it.

But still he couldn't stop. His dick was on fire, ready to erupt, the need to come turning his balls inside out.

"Come for me, Jess. I can't wait much longer." He nipped the back of her neck

Jessa bucked and screamed beneath him, her body trembling as she found her release. Her pussy gripped him like a steel vise, squeezing until he exploded in a rush, his cock pulsing with each blast of semen he shot into her.

"Jessa," he panted, his head resting on her shoulder as they rode the aftershocks of their orgasms.

"Will we ever find this again?" There was no need to elaborate. The sadness in her voice killed him.

"Jess, don't." He eased from her and fell to the side. He couldn't handle words from her while he was still trying to get a grip on his own emotions.

Tomorrow. They'd talk tomorrow.

"It'll be all right, baby. I promise. Everything will be all right." He leaned over and kissed her, his lips lingering over her velvet softness.

It was a promise he hoped like hell he could keep.

CHAPTER SIXTEEN

Jessa spent the better part of the day packing. It should've taken an hour, but she'd been dragging her feet. Closing her packed luggage seemed so...final. As if it signified the end of the happiness she'd found here.

She'd wandered around the suite. The shower, the bath, the bed. The table where they'd eaten, the couch where Garrett had bent her over and shown her a whole new level of sexual gratification. Jessa committed to memory every moment of the last few days.

She'd learned a lot about herself since she'd met him. She'd never known the satisfaction that came with dropping her inhibitions. She'd never trusted a man enough to feel comfortable asking for what she wanted, taking what she'd asked for. Until Garrett.

Her flight in the morning would bring it all to an end. She'd be back in New York and Garrett would be here. She couldn't even think about what would happen when spring training ended. It would be hard enough to know it was over when he was a thousand miles away. It was inconceivable as to what she'd feel once he settled in New York. She wasn't sure her heart would survive seeing him, knowing he was close and not being able to be with him.

What would she do if he found someone else? And he would. He was prime real estate for women in the market. Sexy as sin, young, with an incredible future? Yep, he'd be snatched up in a New York minute.

Jessa laughed quietly at her own pun. It was either that or cry, and she was in no mood to show up for dinner with red, puffy eyes.

Not for the first time, Jessa cursed her dad and his insane need to control her romantic relationships. She'd never let it affect her decisions before, but this time it was different. This time, people could be hurt. Garrett could lose his job.

At this point, she wasn't one-hundred percent sure how her dad would react to her feelings for Garrett. Without that certainty, she couldn't take the chance. Wouldn't. She'd give Garrett up before she risked his future.

Even if it killed her.

Slipping into shorts and a light, fitted T-shirt, Jessa tried to shake the dread she felt at the idea of saying goodbye. After everything they'd shared, she wondered if he'd miss her or not. It would be little consolation to her broken heart either way.

She wasn't ready to say goodbye.

She strode to the bathroom and checked her reflection one last time. Garrett had said casual. He didn't want her dressing up or spending a lot of time getting ready. He liked her as she was, he'd said, calling her a natural beauty.

She hoped he'd meant it. The sides of her hair were pulled up in a clip to keep it out of her face. What little makeup she'd put on gave her skin a subtle glow. It wasn't much more than she'd do for a day at the ballpark. Jessa slid her feet into her favorite pair of sandals and headed to the elevator.

As the floors melted away with quiet beeps, Jessa's nerves tightened. Dinner with Garrett meant goodbyes. He'd said they needed to talk, but she didn't want a big, dramatic scene. She didn't want to cry. She wouldn't be *that* girl.

It was ironic, really. She'd always stayed away from ballplayers. In the romantic sense, anyway. She'd silently supported her dad's mandate that she not get involved. It had been fine with her.

But, nothing about her current situation was fine. She loved Garrett. Once she left here, she was afraid she'd never be whole again.

The hotel had closed the restaurant to non-guests tonight. Not that it did a lot of good, because the place was packed. Understandable, considering the hotel was temporarily home to baseball's finest and the local sports network was here filming interviews.

Jessa hesitated at the entrance and scanned the crowd. She found Garrett at the bar, surrounded by women. By the look of it, they were all vying for his attention. Not that she blamed them. She'd rarely seen him in jeans, but he sure did rock the denim. He'd paired the faded blues with a plain, black T-shirt, giving him that rugged, bad-boy look women went crazy for. And — by the look of the crowd — a few men as well.

"Good evening, Ms. Montgomery."

"Hi," Jessa grinned at the handsome young man.

"Mr. Donovan is expecting you. Your table isn't quite ready yet, but you may join him at the bar if you'd wish. It looks like he's already finished up with his interview."

"Thank you." Jessa looked to see if the guy was wearing a nametag.

"Jeremy, miss."

"Thank you, Jeremy." She smiled in gratitude before glancing in Garrett's direction again, only to find him watching her. His mouth turned up in a slow, sensual smile. It was *that* smile. The *I know what you look like naked* smile. His admirers' curious glances turned predatory, as if she was the one thing that stood between them and Garrett.

Damn straight she was.

Possessiveness clawed its way to the surface, fire burning in her cheeks. She'd like to show them a little something about who held Garrett's attention. Who he kissed. Who shared his pleasure. She was the one with that right. Not any of them.

Her hands curled into tight fists at her sides. She couldn't do this right now. There was no way in hell she could spend the evening pretending she didn't know what he tasted like, didn't know the sounds he made when he was buried deep inside her.

She'd never be able to hide the fact that she loved him.

Oh, God.

She had to regroup before she did something they'd both regret. Like act out her fantasy of kissing him stupid to make a statement to all those women.

Concern marred his expression when she raised her hand, conveying to him with her gaze what he was too far away to hear.

Regret.

It weighed heavy on her heart. She wouldn't trade a moment of their time together. Never that. Regret for the pain of a future without him. A pain that was already piercing her chest.

"Jeremy, would you be so kind as to tell Mr. Donovan that I went back to my room for a bit? I'll touch base with him a little later." Escape seemed her best option. Staying here, watching the other women flirt and tease, wondering who he'd choose after she was gone, was definitely not an option. At least not while Jessa felt the need to bitch slap every last one of them.

"Yes, of course." Jeremy's sympathetic frown tore at her as he walked away to deliver her message.

She needed a drink. A shot of something to warm her belly and soothe her nerves. She kept her eyes on her sandals on the way back to her room. She was in no mood for idol elevator chitchat.

Jessa pulled her phone from her pocket and started a new text. If she knew Garrett, he'd find a way to work himself free to check on her. She quickly typed a message and hit send, satisfied he'd think she'd forgotten some work that she'd needed to finish. She'd bought herself thirty minutes. Maybe an hour. Long enough to get some liquid courage in her so she could face his goodbye.

God, she was pathetic.

Jessa walked into her suite and went straight to the bar. There were so many bottles to choose from. Clear or amber? Red or blue? For the first time in her life, she almost wished she'd drank more. She'd enjoyed the fruity drinks she'd had with Joanna and Amy, but there was no way she could throw together a drink like that.

Whiskey. Garrett drank a glass after dinner a few times. He'd never had more than one, but if he liked it, it couldn't be that bad. She sloshed the amber liquid into a glass and brought it to her lips. She fought back a sneeze as the woodsy smell invaded her nose.

Best to drink it down fast.

She took a steady breath and opened her throat. The fiery liquid singed a path from her esophagus to her stomach. She choked, coughed, and slapped her fist against her chest a few times, to what end she didn't know. No amount of slapping would help the burn of the alcohol or the pain of what was to come.

"Jessa." The deep, familiar voice came from behind her. "You've got some explaining to do."

Jessa screamed, her glass shattering as it dropped to the granite countertop. She whirled, heart in her throat, and stared back at the one person she didn't want to see right now.

* * *

Where the fuck was she going?

Garrett frowned at the young man approaching. He bent his head as the host spoke in hushed tones, relaying Jessa's message about the same time his cell phone buzzed in his pocket.

Garrett stared at his phone, knowing her excuse about work was a ruse. His little princess had the worst poker face he'd ever seen. Pain, confusion, regret. That's what he'd seen in her expression. His gut clenched in anger, knowing she was upset and feeling that somehow, he'd been the cause.

"It sounds like you're on your own," the woman standing next to him said. What was her name? Lisa? Lindsey? He was pretty sure it started with an L.

"Only temporarily, ma'am."

She giggled and Garrett bit back a cringe. God, did he ever think that was cute?

Only when Jessa did it. When he tickled her and she laughed with childlike glee it warmed his heart. But this woman, with her bleach blonde hair and fake nails, this woman struck his nerves. As though she'd pulled her manicured fingernails down a chalkboard.

"That's right, sugar," she cooed. "'Cause Lila is here to keep you company." Like a snake, she wound an arm around his, coiling and pulling him against her.

Lila! He knew it started with an L.

Garrett shifted and raised his arm, effectively disengaging the annoying woman. What was it with these women thinking his body was their personal property? He wasn't a damned animal to be petted at their whim.

They were like leeches and he was getting damned tired of pulling them off every time he turned around.

All he'd wanted was a quiet dinner with Jessa to discuss their future. He should have known better than to expect they'd find privacy outside their room.

He chuckled. He'd been to his own room once in the last forty-eight hours, but not to sleep. Not without Jessa. She'd invited him into her bed and he wasn't going anywhere. Not tonight. If he had his way, not ever. Sharing a bed, feeling Jessa's naked flesh against his as they slept, holding her. He was addicted, plain and simple.

His dick pulsed as he remembered the sight of Jessa bent over the couch, her ass pink and warm from his hand. Her cries of pleasure at each blow, her pussy hot and wet for him. She'd liked it. The slight bite of pain, the wickedness of it all. He'd given her the space to let go of her inhibitions, to free herself from social constructs and enjoy the pleasures of her body, and his.

And she'd been glorious.

Well, wasn't this just fucktastic. Rock-hard pecker and the cause was nowhere in sight. Lila would probably think she'd been the one that made him hard. Christ. He'd never get rid of her then.

He shifted toward the bar, hiding the obvious bulge in his jeans. "Sugar?"

Garrett narrowed his eyes on Lila. "Name's Garrett, ma'am." He shook with the effort to remain polite, his Southern manners ingrained deep. The media in the room also helped to keep his temper in check. Reminded him he was here to do a job. Gave him the focus he needed to hide his irritation behind a smile. "I'm flattered by the attention, and I'd be happy to buy you a drink." He maintained eye contact. "But that's where it ends. You won't get what you're looking for from me. My girl has been delayed, but I promise you, I'll be spending my evening with her."

Just as soon as he could break away from this madness.

Garrett had learned that women appreciated honesty, even if it was at their own expense. Better to keep it real than to have Lila believing she had a chance in hell of getting Garrett in bed. Or, God forbid, that he'd invite her to join him and Jessa. Fuck that. If Lila was looking to get laid, she'd better move on.

There was only one women Garrett wanted.

Running, was she? He'd just see about that. The more he'd thought about it, the more he knew they could make it work.

He'd been over it in his head a hundred times today. Studying it from every angle, working it out with each swing of his bat, each race to the bag as he ran through his drills.

He'd convince Jessa and then he'd convince her dad. TJ was a reasonable man. Garrett would make him see how much Jessa had come to mean to him. Sure, it was fast, but there were some things a person just knew.

And Garrett knew he wouldn't let Jessa go without a fight.

So, let her run. She couldn't, wouldn't go far enough for him not to catch up. And when he did, they were going to get a few things straight.

Starting with who she belonged to.

CHAPTER SEVENTEEN

"Sweet Jesus, Dad!" Adrenaline pushed her heart into overdrive. "You scared the ever-loving crap out of me. What are you doing here?"

She looked around, checking the floor for shards of glass. Feeling relatively safe that she could move without slicing her feet open, she grabbed the wastebasket and pulled it closer.

"I came to see what the hell was going on." His voice was calm. Too calm.

She straightened, hoping she didn't look as guilty as she felt. "What do you mean?"

Not wasting any time, TJ waved a newspaper before slapping it down on the coffee table. "This is what I mean. You want to explain that?" He jabbed a finger at the offending paper.

Time seemed to stand still as Jessa went to the table. She didn't take her eyes off her father as she reached for the paper, gauging his mood.

TJ Montgomery was a large, opposing man. He was usually even-tempered, but Jessa had seen him angry before.

Once.

She'd defied him and snuck out of the house when she was fourteen. It was the first time she'd done anything reckless. A girl at her school had invited her to a party. The girl's parents had been away. Jessa had wanted to fit in. To be accepted.

She should have known better. The girl had only invited her because she'd wanted a pass for her and her friends to get into the restricted areas of the stadium.

Jessa had been used, and it had landed her at the police station when a neighbor, complaining about the noise, had called the police. Her father had been furious that night. His eyes filled with anger and the muscle in his jaw twitched as if it would jump from his skin at any moment.

Kind of like right now.

Dread filled her as she glanced at the paper, instantly recognizing the photo on the front.

Under different circumstances, she'd have been pleased. They looked so happy. Sitting in the bakery, heads huddled close together as they ate from each other's forks. Two young lovers sharing a peaceful moment. One of her happiest memories, immortalized in living color on the front page of the sports section. As innocent as it had been at the time, the picture spoke volumes as to the nature of her relationship with Garrett.

How had she not known about this? Because she'd stayed in all day, away from the ballpark and the media, while she prepared herself to leave tomorrow. That's why.

Did Garrett know about this? He couldn't have. He would've told her, warned her. Something.

There was no way she was getting out of this one. It was damage control time.

"This is nothing." She'd need to be more convincing if she was going to save Garrett's job and her ass.

"Doesn't look like nothing." TJ sat forward on the couch, bracing his forearms against his jean-clad thighs.

"You're the one who told me to keep an eye on him. He had a day off. We went for a drive and ended up at the amusement park." She shrugged, thinking to make light of the situation. "We got hungry."

She took a step back as his cheeks reddened even more.

"Do I look stupid to you? That," he pointed to the paper again, "isn't just being hungry for food." He ran his hands through his hair. "Jesus Christ, Jessa. What have you done? You weren't supposed to distract him. You were supposed to —" He stopped, pressed his lips in a tight line.

"Wait. What?" She dug her fingers into her hips. "What was I supposed to do, Dad?"

He stared her down, unmoving. "Don't take that tone with me, girl."

Jessa's stomach turned as a thought occurred. "Do what, Dad? Answer the question."

His gaze broke, dropping to his lap for a moment. It was long enough. Long enough to know something wasn't right.

"You have to understand, Jessa. Garrett is one of the most important players to hit the circuit in a long time. He's the real deal. Chances of us ever seeing a player of his caliber again are, well, slim to none."

Anger replaced her apprehension. White, hot, liquid fury.

"You can't be fucking serious." She closed her eyes, trying to get a grip on the emotional breakdown she could feel coming. She couldn't deal with this right now. "Please tell me that you didn't send me here to get close to Garrett for the media attention."

"Jessa. You'll watch your language, young lady."

She'd nailed it. The minute the words were out of her mouth, his face changed, his eyes frantic to lock on something other than her. She knew guilt when she saw it. She'd felt enough of it these last weeks to be a fucking expert.

Her laugh lacked any humor. "You whored out your only daughter and you're worried about my language? There is something seriously wrong with your priorities, Dad."

TJ surged to his feet. "I did no such thing!"

Jessa squared off with him. "Are you telling me you didn't send me here to make nice with Garrett? You've warned me off every ball player to ever join your club, yet you send me here to what?" Her voice rose an octave. "To *what*, Dad?"

Her dad matched her stance and his chest rose and fell as he took a deep breath. "You're making too much of this, Jessa," he said after a minute. "You and Garrett are the same age. I like the man, so I thought maybe it would be nice for the two of you to know each other. I thought it would help Garrett feel more at ease his first time out."

His expression passive, his gaze dipped down. There was something he wasn't telling her. Her anger boiled over. Tears formed, blurring her vision. "Then what's the problem? Mission accomplished. We know each other," she spat.

His gaze snapped back to hers. "Maybe a little too well, from the looks of this picture."

"Well, excuse me. You should've been more specific about my job responsibilities."

He didn't acknowledge the sarcasm that dripped from her voice. "What were you thinking? Garrett doesn't need this kind of distraction right now."

"Garrett doesn't? *Garrett* doesn't?" Jessa stuttered, unable to finish the thought. "Is that what this is about? You're worried that *I've* distracted *him*?" Jessa fought against the insecurities that had plagued her whole life.

God, she was such an idiot. No matter what she did, she'd never measure up. She'd tried to be what he'd needed. She'd let him drag her to endless sporting events and business meetings. She'd devoted herself to the game he loved. She'd done it to have a place in her father's life. She'd done it because she loved him. And it wasn't enough.

She wasn't enough. She was a distraction.

"Jessa," her father warned.

"You orchestrated this whole thing. You could have told me, you know? You could have explained what you wanted. Instead, you lied to me. You *used* me."

"Stop it, right now. You're being ridiculous."

"Oh, I'm being ridiculous? And pimping me out to one of your precious ballplayers is rational behavior? I hope that picture gets you the attention you wanted. That it —" she broke off.

Bile rose in her throat as another thought took hold.

Garrett.

Her father's golden boy. The one her father had given advice to. Had he advised him as to why she was here?

Jessa thought back to the day they'd met. The way he'd flirted with her, teased her. Told her she smelled like strawberries. He'd come to her room and kissed her silly.

All on the day they'd met.

Who does that? What was it he'd said that morning in the limo? *"I know all about why you're here."* Oh, God.

She was going to throw up.

* * *

Thirty minutes had passed since Jessa had left the restaurant and Garrett was out of patience. He'd have left fifteen minutes ago if Dan Baker, sportscaster from the local TV station, hadn't stopped and offered to buy him a drink so they could chat about the upcoming season. One drink, Garrett had told him. He hadn't promised not to slam it.

Yes, he was looking forward to the upcoming season. No, he wasn't nervous about playing in the big leagues. Excited, but not nervous. Yes, he was looking forward to playing in New York. The questions were all the same. He'd never been much for the media scene, but his agent had insisted he stop hiding in his room and let people talk to him.

If he'd only known what Garrett had been doing in his room, maybe he'd back off his ass a little. Not that Garrett had any intention of sharing that information. Instead, he'd made nice with the reporter until he couldn't take it any longer. He had to find Jessa.

"Thanks for the drink, Dan." Garrett turned on his barstool and extended his hand, his intent to end this impromptu interview clear.

"Any time, Garrett. I appreciate your time. I know you're a busy man." Dan shook his hand with a smile.

"Yep, gotta run." Garrett slid from his seat. "Next time I'm in Tampa, how about we meet up for dinner?" His agent would love it.

"I'll look forward to it," Dan replied, clapping Garrett on the back.

Garrett laughed, genuinely liking the guy. Under different circumstances, Garrett thought it might be fun to hang out with him.

Another time. 'Cause right now, he was done. Was through waiting.

It took him several minutes to escape the restaurant. There seemed an endless supply of people who wanted a piece of him tonight. He hit the lobby and kept moving. Jesus, would he ever get used to that? It was part of the deal, he knew, but that didn't mean he had to like it. He was a low-profile guy in a high-profile job. He was confident though, that he'd find his groove, a balance between what he wanted and what the world wanted from him.

That was another reason he and Jessa were so perfect together. She knew the business. Hell, she didn't know any other way, having been raised in ballparks. She liked the quiet of their room more than the nightlife of Tampa. He was sure it wasn't just because she thought their time was limited and wanted to make the most of it. They both preferred curling up on the couch to dancing the night away.

God, he made them sound like an old, married couple.

He rounded the corner and stopped dead when Jessa stepped from the elevator. The jean shorts she wore showed off her incredible legs. Toned and tanned, his mouth watered at the thought of licking every inch. He drank her in, content to enjoy the view. She'd exited, only to stand in place, people moving around her as she stared at the floor. Was she mumbling to herself?

Unease washed over him as he approached. Slow. Steady. Wary. "Jess?"

Her head snapped up, her eyes blazing with anger and pain.

Garrett felt it like a sucker punch to his gut. He'd hurt the son of a bitch who'd put that look on her face. And he'd enjoy it too.

Garrett wrapped his hands around her biceps, resisting the urge to pull her to his chest. "Baby, what it is? Was someone bothering you?" He glared around them, searching for anyone who looked in need of a good ass-whoopin'.

She laughed then. Laughed so hard he was forced to release her as she grabbed her stomach and curled over. Male instinct shot off warning bells in his head. Women who laughed like that were on the verge of something ... not fun. He'd seen it before. His sister had laughed like that once after his brother-in-law had been killed. The fallout hadn't been pretty.

"Princess." He moved to wrap an arm around her back, his intent to lead them somewhere more private. Whatever was going on, he was certain she wouldn't want to share it here, in a busy lobby, with a restaurant full of reporters and cameras around the corner.

"Stop calling me that." She jerked away and sneered up at him. "My father knows."

Garrett felt the blood drain from his face. Fuck. He kept his voice low. "What does he know, Jessa?"

"Are you going to stand there and tell me you haven't seen the paper today?"

Garrett didn't appreciate her haughty tone. Frustration fired his temper. Why the hell was she attacking him?

"As a matter of fact, I'm going to tell you that very fucking thing. I've been busy all day, Jessa. Why don't you enlighten me?"

"We made the cover of the sports page."

He took a step back, his brain turning to instant replay. They'd been careful. Hadn't they? How bad could it be?

"Oh, it's bad, Garrett," Jessa said, having read his expression. "Stolen moment of intimacy, New York's newest hotshot feeds boss's daughter pastries." She mocked a headline, adding, "film at eleven."

"Shit." He refused to panic. Drawing on the focus he used on the field, Garrett forced his shoulders to relax, willed down the knot in his throat.

Christ. He should've called TJ the minute he realized his feelings for Jessa. He should've trusted himself for the man he was instead of acting like a complete jackass, forcing them to act as though they'd had no right to be together. For a guy who hated playing games, he'd done a helluva job where Jessa was concerned.

"That being said, it seems my father's main concern is that I've distracted his precious golden boy from his job. Funny, he didn't seem concerned in the least that his golden boy violated his daughter."

"What?"

"You heard me." She crossed her arms over her chest, her jaw set in anger.

"Hold up. You're mad at *me*?" Obviously, TJ's reaction had hurt her, but Garrett didn't see how that was his fault.

He leaned in, putting them nose-to-nose. "If I can't call you princess, then you will damn well stop referring to me as golden boy. And I didn't violate you. I fucking worshipped you."

Her eyes softened a bit before she pushed away from him again. "Did you know?"

Garrett was getting tired of her snapping at him.

He felt as if he'd stepped into an alternate reality. Her eyes shone with unshed tears and damn if it didn't rip his guts to shreds. This isn't how he'd imagined their evening. He wanted her screaming in pleasure, not in anger. And not in the middle of the fucking lobby.

"Did I know what?"

She grabbed his arm, a little too forceful for his liking, and tried to drag him along behind her. "Jessa." He pulled her to a stop, the leash he'd held on his temper loosening. "Slow the fuck down and tell me what the hell is going on. Where's your dad?"

Jessa looked around. "Really, Garrett? You want to do this here? In front of all these people?"

He cursed, realizing they'd drawn attention. He laced his fingers with hers and plastered a smile to his face. "No need to make a bigger scene than we already have. There are meeting rooms down the hall. We can talk there. Can you smile and be nice while we walk over? This place is still crawling with media."

She squeezed his fingers. "Oh, we wouldn't want to make a bad impression, would we? That would defeat the purpose."

He shook his head in confusion and led her back the way he'd come, circling around to the empty conference rooms. He entered the first one he came to, pulled her in, and shut the door. Once he closed the blinds to give them as much privacy as possible, he turned to face her, crossing his arms over his chest. "Well?"

She didn't waste time. "Did my father tell you why I'm here?"

"Other than to babysit?" He pinched the bridge of his nose, tired of this cryptic conversation. "Quit with the twenty questions and spit it out, Jessa. Say what you need to say."

"Fine. It's come to my attention that my father sent me here to do more than oversee your progress. He *planned* the whole thing, Garrett. You and me." Her lip quivered as the tears began to fall.

Garrett shook his head. "That can't —"

"And I think you knew about it."

Garrett didn't move. Ice filled his veins, a chill that turned his spine to steel. She couldn't be serious. After everything they'd shared?

He'd risked everything to be with her and now, she blamed him for something he'd had no part of. Without even asking for the truth.

This is what happens when you play games.

Jessa swiped at her cheeks. "You flirted with me from the first moment we met."

"I'm a friendly guy," he gritted out.

"You came to my room, tempting me with pizza. And you kissed me. Why would you do that, unless you had an ulterior motive?"

His temper broke its leash. "Tempting you with *pizza*? Ulterior motive? Are you listening to yourself, Jessa? You can't possibly believe, first, that your dad would do something like that, and second, that I'd agree to it. What kind of man do you think I am? You think I'd use you like that?"

She took a step back as his voice echoed through the room.

"I think it doesn't matter one way or another." She motioned between the two of them. "We knew this thing between us was temporary. If that picture in the paper gives my dad what he wants — to start your career off with a bang and bring attention to the team — then so be it. No harm, no foul. You don't have to worry about losing your job and I don't have to worry about ... well, anything. Never let it be said that I'm not good at my job."

Before he knew what he was doing, Garrett yanked her to him. She choked back a sob, her nails digging into his chest.

"Just a job, huh?" He gripped her ass, ground his hips against her, letting her feel how hard he was. For her and her sassy little mouth. "Does that feel like a job to you? Even pissed as hell I'm hard for you." He nipped at her ear and she shoved him. Pushed herself away and moved for the door.

"Where the hell do you think you're going," he demanded.

"I'm going home." Anguish bled from her voice. "There's nothing left for me to do here." She glanced over her shoulder.

"Don't worry, Garrett. I'm sure you and my father will be very happy together."

And there was the real reason for this entire argument.

"You've got to be fucking kidding me," he muttered as she opened the door. She was about to walk away from him because she was jealous. Jealous!

The best few weeks of his life reduced to this, this mess. After all the time they'd spent together, she still didn't get it.

Anger and hurt were like acid, burning through his veins, leaving nothing but ash behind.

She'd trusted him with her body, but she didn't trust him with her heart.

He should stop her. Tell her they could figure something out, that it wasn't as bad as she thought. He should tell her he cared about her. Instead, he stood there.

And watched her walk away.

CHAPTER EIGHTEEN

Garrett hurled his glove into the lockers, the action not near enough to satisfy the anger that had been on a slow boil the last month. He needed to kick the shit out of something. He needed to bleed. He wasn't sure it would be enough to mask the pain in his chest, but at this point, he'd be willing to try.

He collapsed onto the bench, his arms resting on his thighs as he contemplated the floor.

How the fuck had he gotten here, to this pathetic version of himself?

Spring training was over and he was headed to New York. The house he'd rented was ready to go, his things moved up last week. His family was safe and secure, as was the farm. He'd handed his mother the deed himself, when she'd come to visit last week. He should've been ecstatic. One less thing for him to worry about. But none of it mattered. He still felt empty.

Jessa.

God, he missed her something fierce.

Sheer will and determination had gotten him through the last four weeks. He'd lost count of the number of times he'd dialed her number. The need to hear her voice almost overriding his fury at her misplaced jealousy and exit from his life.

They weren't done. Garrett had seen the look in her eyes that night. Even through her tears, lust glimmered. The same driving need that tore through him whenever he'd touched her. She was responsive, always responsive, her nipples hard against his chest when he'd provoked her.

She'd been hurt, angry. But, she'd also been aroused. And he'd be the one to give her what she desired.

They weren't done at all. They were just getting started.

It was the only thing that kept him grounded.

Friend, lover, boyfriend … husband. Garrett didn't give a shit about labels. It was inside him. Deep. Powerful. A part of him he hadn't known existed until Jessa.

He loved her with a force so primal, it rocked him.

In two short weeks, she'd become the first person he wanted to talk to in the morning and the last person he wanted to see at night.

And the nights were the worst. When he closed his eyes, her face haunted him. Her hungry cries rang in his ears. Their time together stuck on instant replay in his mind. He'd wake up hard and burning, his hand a poor substitute for the velvety warmth he craved. It was enough to drive a man crazy.

Garrett sighed, scrubbing a hand over his face. *And she left me.*

No. She'd kicked him in the proverbial nuts, blamed him for something he had no control over, and *then* left him.

He could've gone after her. Probably should have. He had every intention of setting her straight, making her see she was wrong about him. Again. If that didn't work, a good, long spanking of that fine ass of hers might do the trick.

Focus, control. These were things he was familiar with. He wasn't used to his emotions being all over the playing field. One minute, he'd wanted to forget her completely. The next, he'd wanted to blow off his job and go after her. Neither were options, leaving him aggravated and feeling helpless. More fuel for his anger.

It was a vicious cycle.

Sonofabitch! He raked his fingers through his hair and ground out a frustrated snarl.

"I see the mood is contagious. There's a lot of that going around." TJ's voice drifted from behind him.

Garrett stiffened, his muscles tightening, flexing as if preparing for a fight.

Just fucking perfect.

"Sir?" Garrett eased to his feet, turning to eyeball Jessa's dad, keeping his expression blank.

Not quite as tall as Garrett, TJ was dressed in a dark blue polo shirt, jeans, and boots. He could've been anybody. No fancy watch, no ten-thousand dollar suit. Nothing to indicate TJ Montgomery was worth billions. Or that he held Garrett's future in the palm of his hands.

"Come with me." TJ didn't wait for an answer as he turned and walked away, leaving Garrett to catch up.

Garrett hesitated a moment, offering nothing more than a shrug to his interested teammates, before following.

They walked through the training area to the rooms at the back. TJ opened a door and peered in before motioning Garrett inside. The med room resembled the one he'd been in with Tyler over a month ago. Felt like eons.

Garrett propped his ass against the counter. He crossed and uncrossed his arms. He didn't want to appear defensive, but damn if he didn't want to get this over with.

TJ paced around the room, finally settling against the exam table in a stance that mirrored Garrett's. "How you doing, son?"

Garrett offered him a passive smile. "Won the last five games. I'd say that's pretty good. I've still got a lot to learn."

"Don't we all." TJ pinned him with a stare. "I'm happy with your performance on the field, Garrett. I hadn't expected any less from you. It's not every day I personally recruit a player. You have a gift." He sighed, his shoulders lowering the slightest bit. "But I'm not here to talk about that."

Of course he wasn't.

"My daughter hasn't spoken a word to me since she left Tampa."

Garrett held his tongue, content to let the silence surround them. If the man had something to say, he could come out with it, without Garrett's help. TJ wasn't the only one Jessa hadn't talked to.

The last month had killed any guilt Garrett had over his relationship with Jessa, leaving only anger and resentment. At himself for allowing things to get this far out of control. At Jessa for not giving him a chance. At TJ for his damned rules.

If the man wanted sympathy, he'd come to the wrong clubhouse.

"I assume from that look on your face she hasn't talked to you either."

"Not a word," he snapped, harsher than he'd intended.

TJ's eyes narrowed, his scowl causing deep lines to form around his mouth. "I know you and Jessa got ... close."

Garrett adjusted the cap on his head and bit his tongue. He still didn't know where this was going, but he figured it wouldn't be productive to tell Jessa's dad that he didn't know shit. Close, his ass. He'd been buried so deep in the paradise of Jessa's body that they'd practically been one person. Wouldn't be productive to share that bit either.

"Feel free to speak your mind. You don't have to hold back. I can see you're angry. Probably hurt, too. You have the same look in your eyes that Jessa's had every time she's looked at me over the last month." His expression turned sad as he shook his head. "I know my daughter, Garrett. And I know you. Why do you think I put the two of you together in the first place?"

"So, it's true then?" Garrett's heart picked up the pace, thrumming in his ears. The line between boss and man blurred as he saw red. He didn't give a good goddamn who this man was. His boss, Jessa's dad, the fucking pope. No one had the right to play with his life, with Jessa's life. No one.

Fuck it. Let TJ trade him. He was damn good at his job. Garrett wouldn't make it to his rental car before the offers started to pour in. He didn't care anymore. He rubbed his shaking hands down his thighs in an effort not to wrap them around TJ's neck.

"Relax, son, and let me explain." His gaze implored him for understanding, but Garrett wasn't feeling all that charitable at the moment.

"Talk."

TJ shook his head with defeat. "I'm sure you're aware by now that Jessa hasn't dated much. I blame myself for that. She should've had a mother. Someone to give her the feminine influence girls need at a young age. Someone to encourage her and to help her understand that not all men are out to, well, you know." He cleared his throat, his discomfort obvious in the strain on his face. "Instead, she had me. A no-nonsense kind of guy who'd rather be at the ballpark than anywhere in the world, even if that meant dragging my young, blossoming daughter all over hell's creation to do it."

"You're the one who warned her away from dating ball players. Tell me, TJ, if she spent all her time in ballparks, who else was she going to meet? Her lack of maternal influence isn't the problem."

"I've made a lot of mistakes. You'll know what I mean someday when you have a daughter. There's no rational thought involved. You'll want to protect her and keep her safe. You'll want to put her in a goddamn bubble."

Garrett didn't need a daughter to understand it. He'd give his life for Georgia Grace. He might only be her uncle, but he could foresee a talk or two with the boys who showed interest in her.

TJ blew out a harsh breath. "I taught her to be strong and independent. But, she doesn't trust people. Guess I taught her that, too. Lord knows I didn't encourage her to develop relationships. I wanted her to be cautious. I didn't want to see her hurt."

"How's that working out for you?"

TJ chuckled, unfazed by Garrett's hostility. "My intentions were honorable, I assure you. My only wish was to see my daughter happy. And she wasn't. She'd closed herself off from the world. All she did was work. So, when you came up, I thought the two of you might hit it off, being the same age and all."

Garrett held on to his temper by the thinnest thread. "You lied to your own daughter. Used her like a fucking puppet master, guiding her where you wanted her to go. Jesus fucking Christ! To what end, TJ? Is she happy now? What makes you any better than anyone else who's tried to use her over the years?"

Surprise filled his expression. "I'm her father."

As if that was enough. "A father who thinks he can plan his daughter's life!" Garrett raged.

TJ's lips thinned. "I wasn't trying to plan her life. I'd hoped she'd find her own way. I put the two of you on the same path, hoping you'd be friends. Jessa needs people her own age to spend time with. I trusted you'd look out for her. I didn't anticipate what happened between the two of you."

"You didn't anticipate." Garrett ripped his cap off his head and sent it hurling across the room, his curse echoing around them. "We're young and single. Jessa is beautiful and you —"

"Whatever happened between you and Jessa was none of my doing, Garrett."

Garrett seethed at the irony. They'd all played an intricate game, hadn't they? TJ may have maneuvered their initial meeting, but he was right. Garrett had made the decision to go along with Jessa about keeping their relationship a secret. For him. He'd agreed in order to protect his own ass when he should've been protecting hers.

TJ wasn't the only asshole in the room.

"I love my daughter, Garrett. I'd never do anything to hurt her."

Garrett blew out a breath. "But you did hurt her, TJ. That's the point. You hurt us both by not being honest." The pain in Jessa's voice was fresh in Garrett's mind, even now. "For the record, she never distracted me. If anything, she kept me focused. How could you blame her for something that didn't happen? Where's the logic in that?"

"Logic doesn't come into play when it's your daughter, Garrett. You don't understand. I never expected Jessa to fall in love with you. I never expected her to fall in love with anyone."

Garrett stared at the man, incredulous. Did he even *know* his daughter? Garrett may not have a long history with Jessa, but even he saw it. Sweet and kind, full of fire and passion. His Jessa was made to love. "Then you're a fool. And she could do worse. At least with me she'd be cherished."

She'd be loved.

There wouldn't be anyone else. Not for him. And as long as Garrett had breath in his lungs, no other man would touch her. Jessa belonged to him and soon, very soon, she'd know it.

"You have every right to be angry."

"You're damn right I do. My relationship with Jessa aside, *you* hurt her. You made her feel like I was more important to you than she is. I don't give a shit how you treat me, but nothing, no one, is more important than Jessa."

TJ's back went rigid, his jaw clenched. "I accept that I didn't handle things well, but Jessa is my daughter. She knows what she means to me."

"Does she? No offense, but from where I stand, there seems to be some confusion."

"I don't follow."

"Let me draw you a fucking map then. How many times have you taken Jessa shopping?"

"What? What does shopping have to do with anything?"

"How many times?" Garrett forced his voice to calm. "Or to get her nails done? Or any other girly thing?"

"Jessa doesn't do those things. We spend a lot of time together. So, I don't take her to the spa —"

"Where do you spend time with her? At a ballpark? At work? At home? And Jessa *does* do those things."

"What are you getting at? I've always treated Jessa like —"

"A son?"

He scowled. "I was going to say like she was the most important thing to me."

"Ah, if Jessa really believed that, then we wouldn't be in this situation, would we? How can you not know this?" Garrett shook his head in shock. "She's always wondered if you'd wished she was a boy. Someone you could raise to be like the men who play for you." He held his palm up, not interested in what was about to come out of TJ's mouth. "It's my turn to talk. Jessa said you blamed her for our relationship. That she was distracting me from my job, which we've already determined is utter bullshit. But did you, even once, give Jessa any indication her welfare was more important to you than my ability to play baseball?"

The idea that TJ believed Garrett wouldn't give his all to the team insulted the hell out of him, but he'd get over it. This wasn't about him.

Confusion, followed by denial, dawned in the man's eyes as Garrett's words hit their mark.

TJ spun away from him, moving across the room. Garrett watched his knuckles turn white as he gripped the edge of the counter, leaned in as though it was the only thing keeping him on his feet. Silence hung heavy in the air as Garrett gave the man space to draw his own conclusions.

"Jessa loves the ballpark."

"She does. But, did you ever give her the choice not to?"

"It's who I am." His voice was so low, so quiet, Garrett almost missed it.

TJ's fist slammed into the counter before he turned back to Garrett, his face filled with regret.

Garrett made an effort not to look smug as he relaxed against the counter. "Exactly. You love her, but you ensured the destruction of your own plan by ignoring her feelings. She walked away from me because of it."

"I'd always worried I'd mess up Jessa's life. Kids don't come with a manual, you know. I tried to be a good father. I should've trusted her. And given her more reason to trust me." TJ slumped into a chair and leaned forward, cupping his face in his palms. "Now, she's miserable."

"Yeah? Well that makes two of us."

TJ looked at him, studied him. "Do you love her?"

"All due respect, sir, any feelings I have or don't have for your daughter are between me and her. Jessa deserves to be the first to know."

Garrett was still pissed. He didn't know if he and Jessa had a future together. But if they did, he was setting the boundaries now. This relationship, whatever it turned out to be, was not a threesome. Garrett would give the man his due as her father, but he wouldn't tolerate any more interference.

TJ scowled. "I respect that. Don't say I like it much, but I respect it. You're a good man, Garrett. I'll trust my daughter is in good hands."

Yes, well. That remained to be seen, didn't it?

Garrett looked TJ in the eye, gave him fair warning. "I'm still angry."

TJ nodded once. "Anger is a funny, vile thing, son. It dissipates. It lessens over time, eventually leaving you all together. Question is, what will it leave you with? A forgiving heart? Or a hole in your gut so vast, you'll never feel complete again?" His hand circled Garrett's shoulder and squeezed, sadness brimming in his gaze. "I'm truly sorry, Garrett. Don't let my mistakes dictate your future. For your own sake, and for Jessa's, don't let anger rob you of the chance for something beautiful."

CHAPTER NINETEEN

Jessa stared at the treadmill.

She knew how this was going to go. Same as every other day for the last four weeks. It didn't matter how far she ran — or for how long — the outcome was always the same.

Mile one. She'd set her stride, working toward a pace she could keep for a while. The rhythmic thud of her shoes against the tread, the low hum of the machine. Nothing could stop her memories of being with Garrett. She'd up the volume on her iPod.

Mile two. Garrett's smile — the one he reserved just for her. The way his tongue eased over his bottom lip, milliseconds before the corner of his mouth curled up. His eyes would darken, his lids would grow heavy with a gaze that said he knew exactly what to do to make her scream. And, sweet mercy, how he'd made her scream.

By mile three, Garrett's hands were on her skin, his mouth licking, biting, tasting every inch of her until mile four, he'd take her. He'd slide his hands over her ass, bend her over that couch again and … mile five she'd give up, frustrated and angry with herself for being such a complete idiot.

So, she stared at the treadmill.

She couldn't outrun her memories any more than she could outrun the pain in her chest. She was in love with Garrett Donovan, and she'd messed it up. The first man who had cared about her. Not her name, not her money or who her father was. Her. The first man she'd trusted, and she'd treated him as if he'd meant nothing to her. Allowed petty insecurities to get in the way of what they could've had together.

Jessa had spent the last month in a hell of her own creation. And it was one she was done living in. She wasn't sure about the old adage that time healed all wounds, but it did give a girl perspective.

She'd blamed and cursed her dad for something she should've been grateful for. His reasons for sending her to Tampa were irrelevant. Once she'd gotten home and the tears had stopped, she'd remembered her dad would never do anything to hurt her. Not intentionally. It seemed Jessa had inherited the overreact gene, along with the gene that included popping off at the mouth before thinking things through. Something she'd done a lot with Garrett, she'd realized.

Perspective.

She'd gone to Tampa to meet Garrett, but what she'd really found was herself. In those two short weeks, Jessa had felt alive, connected, a part of something bigger than the life she'd been living.

Garrett hadn't only been her lover. He'd been her friend. They'd talked, and not just about baseball, although his respect for her opinion about the game made her heart melt a little. They'd talked about family and farming, where the best places were to eat in New York and which were her favorite museums.

They'd argued over who was better at Guitar Hero.

It hadn't mattered that she'd never played before. All that mattered was the mischievous gleam in Garrett's eyes before he'd thrown her over his shoulder — threatening to spank her for arguing with the self-proclaimed Guitar Hero master — and carried her to the bedroom where he'd promised to teach her how to play.

She didn't just want more. She wanted it all. Jessa wanted everything Garrett was, and the person she was when she was with him. He'd shown her the woman she could be. Daring, sexual, loving.

She didn't know if he'd forgive her, but she'd never forgive herself if she didn't try. At the very least, she'd apologize. She owed him that and so much more.

She was through moping around, through running.

Garrett would be in New York by now. He'd play his first game at his home stadium tonight. And she'd be there, but she'd keep out of sight. He'd be nervous enough without throwing a reminder of what she'd done to him in his face. When the game was over, she'd find him. She'd apologize, admit she'd fucked up, and take responsibility. Just as her dad had always taught her.

She prayed it would be enough. She prayed she hadn't lost him.

"Jessa."

Jessa closed her eyes as the deep timbre of his voice caressed her senses. Her overactive imagination was getting the best of her. She'd dreamed about him every night since she'd left. Now, she was hearing him when she was awake? Maybe she was losing her marbles.

"Jess."

The firm demand made her jump. Definitely not dreaming then. She willed her heart to calm as she eased around.

"Garrett." His name came out on a surprised sigh. Seeing him on TV over the last month didn't prepare her for the man who stood in the doorway. He looked different from the last time she'd seen him, but no less handsome. Quite the opposite, in fact. His hair was longer on top and tousled, as though he'd been running his hands through it. His face was tanned, the Florida sun enhancing his already stunning looks. She fought the urge to let her eyes wander as he leaned against the doorframe. "What are you ... how did you —"

"Your dad let me in."

She chuckled. "Of course he did." Her father was meddling again, she was sure. But this time, she didn't mind. He could butt his nose in all he wanted as long as it meant Garrett was here.

"Don't start that shit with me, Jessa." Garrett put a hand up. "And don't say another fucking word. You've had your turn. Now it's mine."

Stunned, Jessa swallowed hard. "Garrett, wait —"

He stalked forward, towering over her, his face set with determination. "I don't think you understood me. You're going to stand there and listen to what I have to say. Without interrupting. Consider this your first warning."

She forced herself to remain still, her eyes locked on his. She deserved his fury, but, at the same time, she couldn't help but wonder about the consequences if she spoke. She blinked with a slight bob of her head and laced her fingers in front of her.

His gaze flickered as if he hadn't expected her easy compliance and Jessa's womb trembled. The man was damn sexy when he was angry, but that wasn't all she saw. Behind the anger, behind the pain she'd caused. It was *her* look.

She bit back a smile, her heart soaring with hope.

"Whatever shit is going on between you and your dad, Jessa, it's got nothing to do with me. I've made mistakes. I should've been more concerned about your feelings than covering my own ass. I'm sorry for that."

She couldn't let him take the blame. "None of what happened was your fault. You don't —"

He put two fingers across her lips. "I wasn't kidding, Jessa."

His gaze was glued to her mouth and she pressed her lips together, signaling she'd be quiet. His fingers lingered, his warmth seeping into her skin. "I should've told you how I felt. What those days with you meant to me." His wrist rotated and he cupped her face, caressing her cheek with his thumb. "I shouldn't have let you walk away. It doesn't make any sense, yet ..." When he spoke again, his voice was soft, seductive. "God, I've missed you."

Her knees trembled with relief, tears forming in her eyes. Garrett was here, touching her again. And he'd missed her. It was a good start.

She pressed her cheek into his hand, basking in the feel of his skin against hers. She shivered as his thumb swiped over her bottom lip.

"I've dreamed of tasting you again."

She parted her lips. "So, do it. Taste me, Garrett." Her body craved to push him, to shatter his control. To stake its claim on him, mark him as hers.

He arched a brow, his fingers teasing, pressure deepening as he eased around to cup her neck, massaging the tension away.

She groaned and rolled her head as her muscles loosened, relaxed under his touch. Jessa lifted her chin, offering him her lips, her neck, any part of her he wanted.

Garrett's hand slid up, his fingers winding around her ponytail. She gasped, tiny sparks erupting across her scalp as he jerked her head back. Crystal blue fire burned in his eyes.

"I swear on all that's holy, Jessa. If you ever do anything like that to me again, I'll paddle your ass so hard, you won't sit for a week."

* * *

His control snapped.

Jessa relaxed against him, her body melting into his. Nothing in the world could've kept him from pressing his lips to hers. From forcing her mouth open, shoving his tongue inside and taking what he'd been dying for.

Like throwing gasoline on a fire, hunger exploded inside him, stealing his ability to breathe, to think about anything except getting inside her. Possessing her.

The power of it shook him.

He wrapped an arm around her waist and hoisted her up. He feasted on her lips, taking what she'd offered and demanding more.

Four fucking weeks.

He hadn't intended to ravish her. Not until he'd gotten some things off his chest. But the second she'd sighed his name, as if the word itself was pure pleasure in her mouth, his will to talk vanished, replaced by a driving force he couldn't contain. A need that had been burning him, eating at him, since the moment she'd walked out.

His chest heaved as he tore his mouth from hers. "We aren't done talking."

"Can't we be done for an hour or so?"

His shaft fought to bust the seams of his pants. "Eager, are we?" Why yes, yes he was.

She lowered her gaze to the floor. "I'm sorry, Garrett. For so many things."

The pain in her voice killed him. It was a tone he never wanted to hear again. He cupped her head and pulled her in, holding her close. Willing her to feel the emotions raging within him.

She shuddered with a sob. "I thought I'd lost you."

"Hey, hey. Shhh. It's okay, baby. Don't cry." He rubbed her back, his cheek resting against the top of her head. Any anger he'd felt evaporated the second he'd seen her. She looked gorgeous in her tiny running shorts and sports top, both leaving more skin exposed than covered. But, her eyes were drawn, dark circles shadowed her face as if she'd not slept since he'd last seen her. And she was thinner. The soft contours of her body sculpted into harder lines. He glared at the treadmill, wondering how many hours she'd spent on the damn thing. Running. From him.

She wasn't running now. And even if she did, he'd go after her. He'd let her walk away from him once. Wouldn't happen again.

"You haven't lost me, princess. I'm here, and I'm not going anywhere. Unless it's to find a more appropriate place to get you naked."

She laughed and wiped her eyes. "That works for me." She threw her arms around his neck and hopped, wrapping her legs around him.

Garrett bit the inside of his mouth as the heat from her core bounced against him. His fingers dug into her ass as she shamelessly rocked her hips.

If he didn't find a bed in the next thirty seconds, he'd take her right here on the floor.

Jessa nuzzled his neck as he moved them to the hallway and hesitated. The house she shared with her father wasn't as large as he'd expected, but it was still huge.

"Which way?"

She looked confused, her eyes darting left, then right.

He slipped his fingers under the seams of her shorts and groaned at the hot, velvety softness that greeted him. "You don't know where your room is?"

She nipped at his bottom lip. "You're distracting me. Go left."

He turned and strode in the direction she'd indicated. He went into the first room he came to.

"This is a guest room," she informed him.

"Well, I'm a guest. It's got a bed and a door. Right now, that's enough. And tough shit for anyone who walks in if that door doesn't have a fucking lock on it. You're lucky we made it this far."

He dropped her on the bed and jerked her shorts down her legs.

"Garrett! You have a game tonight!"

"We've got plenty of time."

He pushed the door shut, thanking God there was indeed a lock. Within seconds, Garrett had Jessa naked and sprawled on the bed. She cupped her breasts, teasing the dark, beaded tips while he kicked off his shoes. Grabbing the back of his collar, he yanked the shirt over his head and let it fall to the floor.

He slowed his movements, caught in the spell of Jessa's sultry smile as she played with her breasts. He unbuckled his belt, leaving it in the loops as he worked the button of his jeans.

The vixen arched her hips, raised her ass clear off the bed to tease him with the glistening pink flesh between her thighs.

"You've got a lot to make up for, Jessa. Tell me ... how sorry are you?" She yelped when he jerked her ankles, pulling her to the edge of the bed. "Stand up."

Her skin flushed a pretty pink. Her breasts trembled with every breath. She was the most beautiful woman he'd ever seen as she stood before him, eyes heavy and dark, her pupils dilated with lust. Each subtle nuance gave away her desire.

He couldn't wait another second. His jeans had become painfully tight and he ached for the sweetness of her mouth. Garrett pressed against her shoulders, letting her know where he wanted her.

She dropped down, resting her palms against his thighs and

gazing up at him with an innocent gleam. "I'm very sorry, Garrett." She leaned in and rubbed her cheek against him.

He drew in a breath, the sight of her on her knees a powerful aphrodisiac. His chuckle was deep with sensual promise. He pinched her chin, raising her gaze to his. "Did you touch yourself this last month, baby? Did you pet that sweet pussy and think of me?"

Her eyes flared. "Yes," she breathed. "Did you?" She put her mouth against him, her breath burning through the fabric. "Jack off, I mean."

A growl was forced from his chest as he bent to capture her mouth. "Every goddamned day. It wasn't enough, Jessa. It wasn't near enough." He plunged his tongue past her lips, savoring her soft, sweet moans. She met him stroke for stroke, her tongue swirling, tangling with his.

She yanked at the zipper of his jeans and he straightened, pulled back. She rested her hands on her legs while he stripped his pants off. "God, Jessa, you turn me until I don't know which way is up. You're so fucking sexy sitting there, waiting for me."

She licked her lips and smiled. "You're pretty fucking sexy yourself."

He tapped the insides of her thighs with his foot, coaxing her open. "Spread your knees, Jess. I want to see how wet you are. I'll bet you'll get even wetter as you suck me, won't you, princess? It's going to be so good."

He squeezed the swollen head of his cock and swiped his finger over the moisture that beaded there. He brought his finger to her mouth and she opened, licked the tip, and sucked him in. All the way to his palm. She wrapped her hand around his shaft and Garrett reveled in the pleasure of her touch.

He pulled his finger from her mouth and reached for the band that held her hair. He yanked it free, releasing the silky tresses he loved so much. He loved everything about her.

Garrett forced his hips still when she kissed the head of his cock, her tongue teasing the slit. He tightened his grip on her head. "That's it, baby. Take me inside those pretty lips. Ah, fuck. Jessa."

She sucked him deep, her moan vibrating through him as he fought off his release.

Four fucking weeks he'd been without her. Had dreamed about this very thing, her mouth an inferno around him. He fisted his hands in her hair and pumped his hips in short, shallow strokes. She fought to take him deeper, but he held firm, wanting to prolong the pleasure.

Her nails dug into his thighs, scraping upward until she reached his sac. He tensed for a moment, waiting to see what her wicked hands would do next. A sound tore from his chest, pure animalistic need, as she trailed a nail across the sensitive tissue behind his balls.

"Ah, Christ. Jessa."

She used his distraction to suck him to the back of her throat, working him until his legs shook with the effort not to come. Sweat ran down his face. It took everything he had to remain standing.

She freed him with a snarl that surprised him. "I can feel you holding back, Garrett. No more. It's just you and me, remember? No more secrets, no more running. I want your taste in my mouth, Garrett. I want to drink every ounce of you." She stroked him as she spoke. "Let me have it, Garrett."

She pushed her mouth back on him and he couldn't hold out. The need to give her what she wanted overrode all other thoughts in his head. He took control, holding her steady as he fucked her mouth. His spine tingled as she reached up to cup his testicles.

"Shit," was the only thing he could say as the most violent orgasm he'd ever experienced slammed into him. He pumped his hips, his seed erupting into Jessa's mouth. She lapped, swallowed and held on, milking him until he shuddered, his dick so sensitive, he didn't think he'd survive the sensation of pulling out of her.

His legs shook with the aftermath, jerked when she released him. She'd never looked more beautiful as she licked her lips with a content, happy smile.

Mine.

He ran a hand over her hair. His emotions hit him hard, square in the chest. He stared down at the woman who'd changed his life. "I love you, Jessa."

CHAPTER TWENTY

Jessa wasn't sure she'd heard him correctly. He loved her?

Her first instinct was to blow it off. Blame his words on the orgasm she'd given him. People say things they don't mean in the throes of passion, right?

No. Not her Garrett. And she'd never doubt him again.

He pulled her across his lap as he collapsed on the edge of the bed. And he did collapse, as if his legs had no strength left. She felt a gust of female satisfaction that she'd done that.

This big, gorgeous, wonderful man loved her. She kissed his chest, directly over his pounding heart. She kissed his collarbone, trailing her lips over the contours of his shoulder. Her fingers traced the hard lines of his bicep, as her mouth worked up his neck. She nipped his earlobe, felt his breath hitch as she trailed her tongue over the sting.

"I love you, Garrett," she whispered into his ear.

After a declaration like that, Jessa expected him to devour, take control of her passion as he had before.

Not this time.

He captured her mouth. He lingered, his tongue savoring her as if he had all the time in the world. Exploring her mouth.

Breathing new life into her.

His was a slow, steady seduction of her senses. He laid her out on the bed, crawling over her like a predator about to take his prey. "You're mine, Jessa."

He teased her breasts with his fingertips, feathering over her skin.

"Yes, Garrett. Yours," she breathed, "all yours."

She wiggled, trying to encourage him to touch her nipples. Dying for him to touch her. Arousal unlike any she'd ever felt surged through her, made her ready to beg.

He moved slowly, leaving her breasts to trail down her stomach, over her sides. He touched every inch of her, using only his fingertips, dusting over her skin until even the slightest whisper made her lose her mind.

He heightened her awareness of her own body. Everywhere he touched, she ached. Her nipples were painfully hard and her pussy was drenched in need.

And he progressed on, ignoring all the obvious places. Ramping her arousal as well as her frustration. Minutes seemed like hours as he played on her skin.

She cried out when he kissed the inside of her thigh. First one, then the other. Lick, kiss, nibble. So close. So close to where she needed him. His fingers trailed over her hips, down the outside of her legs as he positioned himself at her apex.

Jessa saw stars as he blew a stream of hot air over her sex. "You're killing me, Garrett. Please. Do something."

His husky chuckle made her muscles clench unbearably tighter. "I am doing something, princess. I'm loving you."

"Can you love me a little faster then? I'm about to burst into flames here."

"Not until I get inside you. I want to feel you burst around me."

He stroked his tongue through her slit and Jessa cried out at the sensation. "God, please, Garrett. Please. I can't take anymore."

He came over her and pressed his lips to hers. Her taste mingled with his as he wrapped his arms around her and rolled them until she straddled his hips.

She braced her hands on either side of him and rocked back and forth, coating his very hard, very thick erection with her juices. Sparks of electricity shot through her as she rubbed her tortured nipples against his chest.

Garrett stilled her with a hand to her hip. "Climb on, princess.

Ride me. Take us where we need to go."

"Take what's mine." She rose up and he tucked the head of his shaft against the opening of her pussy.

"Damn straight."

Jessa sank down, taking him all the way to the hilt. Her pussy stretched, burned, as she fought to adjust to his penetration.

She dug her nails into the hard plane of his chest, the muscles bunching under her palms. She glanced down at him. Love and lust intermingled, giving him a wild, ravenous look. He was breathtaking. She knew this was where she belonged. With Garrett. To Garrett.

"I love you," she said as she started to move. Slow at first, then faster as she found a rhythm sure to drive them both over the edge.

He palmed her breasts, pinching and rolling her nipples, giving her what she needed. He always knew what she needed.

Her legs trembled and she worked herself up and down on his length, the exquisite feeling of being in love second only to having him inside her.

"I love you. Damn it, Jessa, I love you so fucking much." He grabbed her and rolled them again, seizing control.

It was as if the words broke something free inside them as he put her ankles against his shoulders and pounded into her. It was more than the act of having sex. More than making love.

The world around them blurred as she relinquished her fears and doubts. She'd given her heart to this man. Her heart and her soul. And she knew everything was going to be all right.

She screamed as her orgasm crashed over her, blinding her. Her womb pumped, her pussy seized, and Garrett yelled out. Her body contracted again as his hot semen filled her. Tiny aftershocks resonated as he slowed his hips, exhaustion claiming them both.

Garrett rested his forehead against hers as they both fought to breathe. He grumbled as he eased out of her and rolled over on his back next to her.

"That was ..." She was without words.

"Jesus, I think I'm dead." Garrett slapped a palm to his chest.

Jessa laughed. "Right there with you."

They lay together, the smell of sex and sweat an erotic mixture in the aftermath of their lovemaking. They didn't speak right away. Didn't need to. Their bodies had said it all.

After a while Garrett reached out, curling her into his side. "What's going on in that head of yours?"

Jessa burst out laughing. "After recovering from your spectacular lovemaking skills, I was thinking about your game tonight."

Garrett grinned. "Spectacular, huh? So spectacular that you're thinking about my game?"

She giggled as he grabbed her ribs and tickled her. "Garrett!" She squirmed in his embrace. "Stop!"

He let her go, easing himself from the bed. "While we're on the subject, I know you have a life and a job here. I'd be lying if I said I didn't want you with me. This last month was torture, Jessa. If we have to be apart, promise me it won't be for long periods of time."

He tossed her top to her and she wiggled it on. "You want me to travel with you?"

"Of course I do." He shoved a leg into his jeans.

She wrinkled her nose at him. "Are you sure you aren't trying to get out of traveling with the other players?"

He frowned. "You think I'd try —"

"It was a joke, Garrett." She scooted from the bed, found her shorts and pulled them on. "I'm not sure I could travel with you all the time, but I'd love to be there with you when I can."

He nodded, seemingly content with her answer as he finished buckling his belt. "You'll be there tonight?"

"I wouldn't miss it. How's Sandquist looking to take over for Tyler?" She knew the stats, but she wanted to hear from Garrett firsthand what his thoughts were.

"He's not Tyler, but he'll get the job done. We've played well together the last few weeks."

"They're going to be gunning for you tonight. Malone is famous for trying to show up the rookies." She bent to pick up his shoes. "With your record, he'll be even worse. He'll want to make an example of you."

Garrett laughed and wrapped his arms around her from behind. "Nervous, baby?"

She tilted her head, giving him access to her neck. "Maybe a little. If he throws at you, I may not be able to hold my tongue."

He squeezed her. "My little fireball. Let me worry about Malone." He nipped at the muscle between her shoulder and her neck. "And your tongue."

"Ha ha."

"It'll be fine, Jessa. Stop worrying." He reached in his pocket. "I'd be able to concentrate better if I knew you were gonna be waiting for me after the game." He dangled a key from his finger. "What do you say, princess? Meet me at my place after?"

"Let me guess." She took the key from him. "You want me waiting, naked and in your bed?"

149

He shrugged. "Or fully clothed at the kitchen table with a beer. Or curled up on the couch watching a movie. As long as you're there, that's all that matters to me."

Tears formed at the sincerity in his voice. She swallowed hard. God, she loved this man. He was almost too good to be true, and he was all hers. "I may even make you something to eat."

"Don't get your hopes up, princess. I've barely had time to settle in, let alone stock the fridge. I've gotten the necessities, but you may want to bring any extra stuff that you need."

"Stuff? Like what?"

He kissed her nose. "You know, like that delicious smelling shampoo you use. Toothbrush. Clothes. Shoes. Whatever else you need."

He teased her mouth with his lips, driving her to distraction. They'd never make the game if he didn't stop touching her. "That's a lot of stuff, Garrett. How long are you planning to keep me?"

He gifted her with a wicked grin. "Forever, Jessa." He pressed his lips to hers in a kiss that left her breathless. "I'm keeping you forever."

<<<<>>>>

Parker Kincade is an award-winning erotic romance author of the Martin Family Series.

Her first novel, *One Night Stand*, won the category of Best Erotic Romance in the Celtic Hearts Romance Writers Golden Claddagh contest and was named finalist in the Romance Writers of America/Passionate Ink Stroke of Midnight contest.

Parker lives in the southern United States with her husband, children and beloved boxer sidekick. She loves reading, playing golf, spending time with her family and friends, ice cream from the ice cream truck, taking her dog to the park and watching old musicals.

Find Parker Kincade Online:
    http://www.parkerkincade.com
    http://www.parkerkincade.blogspot.com
    http://www.facebook.com/parkerkincade
    http://www.twitter.com/parkerkincade

ALSO BY PARKER KINCADE

The Martin Family Series:
One Night Stand

Anthologies:
Lucky's Charms

Game On Series:
Spring Training

Next expected title in series:
Southern Heat

Made in the USA
Charleston, SC
12 June 2013